Praise for Beth Vrabel's *Pack of Dorks* and *A Blind Guide to Stinkville*

"Debut author Vrabel takes three knotty, seemingly disparate problems—bullying, the plight of wolves, and coping with disability—and with tact and grace knits them into an engrossing whole of despair and redemption. . . . Useful tips for dealing with bullying are neatly incorporated into the tale but with a refreshing lack of didacticism. Lucy's perfectly feisty narration, emotionally resonant situations, and the importance of the topic all elevate this effort well above the pack."

—*Kirkus Reviews*, starred review

"Lucy's growth and smart, funny observations entertain and empower in Vrabel's debut, a story about the benefits of embracing one's true self and treating others with respect."

—*Publishers Weekly*

"Vrabel displays a canny understanding of middle-school vulnerability."

—*Booklist*

"Lucy's confident first-person narration keeps pages turning as she transitions from totally popular to complete dorkdom in the space of one quick kiss. . . . Humorous and honest."

—*VOYA*

"This book doesn't soft-pedal the strange cruelty that kids inflict on one another, nor does it underestimate the impact. At the same time, it does not wallow unnecessarily. . . . The challenging subject matter is handled in a gentle, age-appropriate way with humor and genuine affection."

—*School Library Journal*

"*Pack of Dorks* nails the pitfalls of popularity and celebrates the quirks in all of us! An empowering tale of true friendships, family ties, and social challenges, you won't want to stop reading about Lucy and her pack . . . a heartwarming story to which everyone can relate."

—Elizabeth Atkinson, author of *I, Emma Freke*

"A book about all kinds of differences, with all kinds of heart."
—Kristen Chandler, author of *Wolves, Boys, and Other Things That Might Kill Me* and *Girls Don't Fly*

"Beth Vrabel's stellar writing captivates readers from the start as she weaves a powerful story of friendship and hardship. Vrabel's debut novel speaks to those struggling for acceptance and inspires them to look within themselves for the strength and courage to battle real-life issues."
—Buffy Andrews, author of *The Lion Awakens* and *Freaky Frank*

"Beth Vrabel weaves an authentic, emotional journey that makes her a stand-out among debut authors."
—Kerry O'Malley Cerra, author of *Just a Drop of Water*

"Most commendable is Vrabel's focus on compromise and culture shock. Disorientation encompasses not only place and attitude but also the rarely explored ambivalence of being disabled on a spectrum. Alice's insistence that she's 'not that blind' rings true with both stubbornness and confusion as she avails herself of some tools while not needing others, in contrast to typically unambiguous portrayals. Readers who worry about fitting in—wherever that may be—will relate to Alice's journey toward compromise and independence."
—*Kirkus Reviews*

"Brimming with wit and heart, *A Blind Guide to Stinkville* examines the myriad ways we define difference between ourselves and others and asks us to reexamine how we see belonging."
—Tara Sullivan, award-winning author of *Golden Boy*

"*A Blind Guide to Stinkville* is a delightfully unexpected story with humor and heart. Vrabel tackles some tough issues, including albinism, depression, and loneliness, with a compassionate perspective and a charming voice."
—Amanda Flower, author of the Agatha Award–nominated *Andi Boggs* series

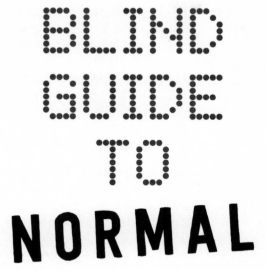

NORMAL

Also by Beth Vrabel

Pack of Dorks
A Blind Guide to Stinkville
Camp Dork

A BLIND GUIDE TO

NORMAL

BETH VRABEL

Sky Pony Press
New York

Sky Pony Press books may be purchased in bulk at special discounts for sales promotion, corporate gifts, fund-raising, or educational purposes. Special editions can also be created to specifications. For details, contact the Special Sales Department, Sky Pony Press, 307 West 36th Street, 11th Floor, New York, NY 10018 or info@skyhorsepublishing.com.

This is a work of fiction. Names, characters, places, and incidents are either the products of the author's imagination or used fictitiously.

Sky Pony® is a registered trademark of Skyhorse Publishing, Inc.®, a Delaware corporation.

Visit our website at www.skyponypress.com.

10 9 8 7 6 5 4 3 2 1

Library of Congress Cataloging-in-Publication Data is available on file.

Cover design by Laura Klynstra
Cover illustration by Chris Piascik

Print ISBN: 978-1-5107-0228-8
Ebook ISBN: 978-1-5107-0229-5

Printed in the United States of America

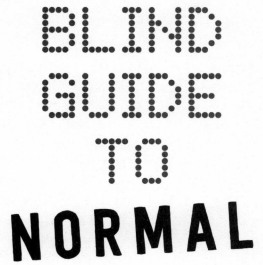

NORMAL

To Goldie, my papaw's long-passed devil cat, for inspiring the General. It almost makes up for the lifelong fear of exposed ankles while walking down stairs.

Chapter One

Even *I could* see that the cake was one twisted joke.

As my friend Alice pushed a cart to the front of the classroom, everyone else backed off, distancing themselves. And since this was a room full of kids attending Addison School for the Blind, it also clued me in that they all had seen the cake before Alice wheeled it in.

Brad (all of our teachers at Addison insisted on being called by their first names) moved the projector so it blew up an image of the cake onto the wall. He read aloud the words set in red icing: "Good luck, Ryder! I'll miss you."

Alice broke in, "But it's really 'Eye'll miss you.' E-y-e!" She snorted at her own joke.

Quiet fell across the room like a blanket.

"Eye," Alice added in a whisper, her usually white-as-paper cheeks pinking as the silence thickened. She stepped closer to me. When I knew she could see, I slowly shook my head, like I was so disappointed. "Um,"

1

she continued, face flaming, "sort of like how you only have one eye . . ."

"That's just sick."

Alice squirmed and I couldn't hold it in another second, laughter ripping out of me. The worst torture in the world is forcing some poor fool to explain a joke. I took off my glasses and pretended to wipe the lens with one hand. After a second, I popped out my fake eye with my other hand. "If you're going to miss it, Porcelain, I could just leave it behind."

Alice slapped away my hand. But she couldn't stay mad at me. No one can. It's a gift. Soon she was laughing even harder than I, making everyone join in. No one can resist Alice's laughter. I guess that's sort of her gift.

"He's holding his eye, isn't he?" asked Lucas, who had started at Addison School in sixth grade like me. But where I was about to head back to public school for eighth grade—hence the going-away party—Lucas would probably graduate from Addison. I, at least, have mild to low vision out of one eye. Lucas was born totally blind.

"Yup, he sure is," Alice said. Although she is technically blind due to albinism, Alice usually just had to get close to something to make out what was going on around her. I smiled, a little pumped that she and Lucas had each other. Thanks to me. I kind of took Alice under my wing when she arrived at Addison a year ago. At first, I just liked making her blush—calling her Porcelain because of her pale skin and stuff like that—but we quickly became friends. Best friends, actually.

Alice and Lucas, however . . . well, Lucas slipped his hand into hers like he could hear my thoughts.

"Speech! Speech!" chirped Lucas, raising their joined hands in a little rally punch.

Alice picked up the chant. "Speech! Speech!"

"All right!" I groaned, but, you know, eating up the attention anyway. I cleared my throat. "My dear people! I don't know half of you half as well as I should like; and I like less than half of you half as well—"

"Hey!" Brad interrupted. "That's Bilbo's farewell speech!"

"Told you I was paying attention in reading class, Teach."

"Too bad you couldn't recall lines like that during the exam," he volleyed back.

"Wow, Brad. Just when you're getting good at these witty comebacks, I'm off. I expect the rest of you to keep him on his toes." I cleared my throat again. Suddenly, looking around at my friends, I couldn't swallow right. "Seriously, though. Thanks for this, guys. Try to hold it together without me. Someone will need to keep an eye out for the newbies."

"But not literally!" added Alice, slicing into the cake. "Shall I save the pupil for you?"

"Absolutely." I grinned like a fool and passed out slices of my giant farewell eyeball cake.

"Going to miss me, Porcelain?" I asked Alice later. We were waiting by the curb in front of the main building for her mom to pick her up. Where most of the kids—like me—boarded at Addison, Alice lived less than an hour away, so she went home each afternoon. Usually we joked around and rehashed our day while waiting for Alice's mom, but knowing it was the last day of school—and my last day at Addison—made it feel sort of awkward.

All around us people were lugging bags to the sidewalk. Parents were pulling up with their hazard lights on, honking horns, and calling out names. I guess it was like any last-day-of-school pickup, except for the clicking of canes against the sidewalk. Alice folded up hers and rested it across her knees as we sank down to sit and wait.

"Of course, I'll miss you," she said. "But you're going to text me every day, right?"

"Right." I beamed a huge grin across my face.

"You know if you don't stop smiling like that a fly's going to land on your tongue."

"I can't help it," I said. "I'm just so . . . I don't know. I can't wait for next year, to get back to normal. Be surrounded by normal—" I bit off the stupid thing I was going to say but it was too late. Alice's face flushed again but not from embarrassment. Man, I can be such a jerk sometimes. "Alice, I didn't mean it like that . . ."

She sighed. "I know. Being here, it makes me forget sometimes. Makes me think I'm normal."

"You are normal! You're *totally* normal! You're like the most normal, run-of-the-mill person—"

"That hole you're digging is getting deeper." Alice laughed. "Besides, I don't think normal exists."

"I shouldn't have used the word *normal,*" I said quietly. "I just meant regular. I'm excited to go to a regular school."

"You don't think it's going to be hard?"

I shrugged. "A little, I guess."

Alice nodded. "You know, it's strange. A year ago, I was so mad that my parents were making me check out this place. I was sure I didn't need it. Now, I get the same nervous feeling when I even think about going back to Sinkville Public. And that's the school in my town! Where I know everybody! Here you are, moving to a new town and not scared at all."

"Well, when you put it that way, my palms get a little sweaty." I knocked into her shoulder with mine so she'd know I was joking.

I guess most people would be nervous in my situation. My parents are research biologists. Mom specializes in entomology (you know, bugs) and Dad in wildlife (anything with vertebrae, but he loves buffalo the most). They travel all over America for assignments that can last anywhere from three months to a year or more. Since I've been at Addison, I usually join them wherever they are for the summers. It can get a little lonely, like when we were tenting it in Idaho. Spring Break was pretty awesome, though. Mom nailed a spot in Hawaii. I came back with a killer tan, even though Alice pelted me with stats about skin cancer.

The whole albinism thing keeps her perpetually smelling like coconuts from all the sunscreen she coats on. Even now, though it was a cloudy afternoon, she wore a wide-brimmed hat and sunglasses, and I still sniffed that faint coconut odor.

"It's Dad's turn for an assignment this summer," I said. "So I'll be four-wheeling across three-point-six million acres of public land in the middle of Nowhere, Wyoming. But Mom says she's a shoo-in for an office research spot in Washington, DC, after this gig, so I can go to a real school in the fall."

"That's great," Alice said, but I could tell she didn't mean it, really.

"Worried you're going to miss me?"

"A little, I guess." She smiled as she copied my words. "I just hope everyone at your 'normal' school can see what a great person you are."

"Why wouldn't they?" I threw out my hands in a what's-not-to-love sort of way. I elbowed her as her mom's car pulled up in front of us.

"You're going to be fine," she said, but I think she was trying to convince herself more than me. Alice isn't always the most confident of girls.

Mrs. Confrey waved from behind the front seat. She looked like a taller, more elegant Alice, only with a curtain of black hair instead of Alice's white locks. "Hey, Ryder! Alice, hurry up! We're meeting your dad for milkshakes."

Alice almost knocked me over, throwing her arms around me in a huge hug. "Bye, Ryder," she whispered, her voice catching.

"Hey, doll, knock it off. I'm going to text you. And I'm sure you and Lucas will meet loads of new friends next year."

"Yeah, but none of them will be as easy to find in a crowd," she said, ruffling up my hair with her hand. Alice confessed a couple months ago that when she started going to Addison the only reason she kept talking to me was that, thanks to my bright red hair, I was the only person she recognized in the hallways. She got up and started to walk away then doubled back. "Ryder?"

"Yeah?" I asked, turning my head to see her better.

"Don't call the girls 'doll' at your new school, okay?" She said it in a rush.

I leaned back on my elbows, squinting up at her. "Are you jealous or something?"

Alice puffed out of her nose like a bull. She crossed her narrow white arMs. "No, dimwit. It's just not something I think you're going to be able to get away with at your *normal* school."

I grinned. "I am who I am, *doll.* This cheetah isn't going to change his spots."

Alice nibbled on her bottom lip until her mom honked the horn again. "Most guys don't say things like that, too, about cheetahs and spots."

I shrugged. Whatever, you know? I was unique. And, all right, maybe spending most of my life cracking up my folks instead of other kids made me more of a wordsmith than most guys my age. They'd catch up.

Alice waved until she couldn't see me anymore as her mom drove away. On the way back to my dorm, where I still had to pack, a couple dozen people stopped me for fist-bumps, wished me luck, and promised to stay in touch.

It should've hit me then—being celebrated like a departing rock star. I should've realized.

Because here's a joke for you (only it's really a joke *on* me): Where can a cocky, one-eyed ginger be the coolest cat around?

Punchline: Only at a school for the blind.

Chapter Two

Here's another joke. Not one of my finest, but it'll do: What did my dad say at the end of a summer of watching elk herds in Wyoming, as he dropped me off at his father's so he could research buffalo in Alaska?

Bison.

Get it? Bye, son. I know. Bad joke. Even worse when it reflects real life.

"I know it's not ideal, Ryder," Mom murmured from the front seat as she shifted the car to park in front of Gramps's house.

"I don't even *know* him." I could hear the whine in my voice but Mom didn't squash it like she normally does. She let out a long breath through her nose instead. I read somewhere that if people spend too much time with their pets, they start to look like each other. I think it's got to be true for researchers and their subjects, too. Mom has huge eyes, a round face, and a tiny thin-lipped smile, plus vibrant red hair always pulled into a tight bun on top of her head. In other words, she's like a mom-sized ladybug.

Next to her, Dad grumbled. He had tight brown curls covering his head with a bushy mustache topping his lip. More hair curled out under the neckline of his chest. He was wide as two average-sized dads and could hike for sixteen hours straight without a break—or the understanding that others (such as, I don't know, his kid) might need one.

"You and your mom will get along just fine with your grandfather," Dad boomed. "You remind me a lot of him."

I tried not to take that personally. After all, Dad left home for college when he was seventeen and never came back. He calls his dad once in a while, but it wasn't not like we saw each other at holidays or anything.

In fact, I hadn't seen Gramps since I was seven, right after the surgery I had to remove my eye. He stayed up all night in the hospital bed next to me, telling terrible knock-knock jokes and watching awful television shows until I laughed. Then he patted my head and left.

"It's very gracious of him to take us in," Mom said.

I don't know how to describe the noise that pushed out of my lungs, but it got my point across. Mom squeezed shut her eyes and rubbed at them with the heel of her hand. "You know this is a great opportunity for your dad. A time when his research really could make a difference! And steering this project in DC is going to mean a lot of late nights for me. Moving in with your grandfather is the best solution for all of us."

Here was the deal: That summer-long research project in Wyoming was supposed to be followed-up with a laboratory research job for Mom in the DC area, right? Everything was going on track. Heck, I even got to man a four-wheeler one memorable occasion. (Imagine driving with your foot pressed solid against the gas while a crazy elk charges you over roots and rocks. Now close one eye.)

Then Dad went and got an offer for a yearlong assignment in Alaska. The untamed wilderness part of Alaska. You know, the part without schools. Without buildings, really. This is where Dad always wanted to study, ever since, as Mom put it, I was knee-high to a grasshopper. And Mom? You'd think she would've been on my side. After all, it was supposed to be her turn on the schedule and she worked hard to nail that cushy office job in Washington. Sure, I had a hard time picturing my always-on-the-move dad biding his time in some urban place. But it still stung a little how quickly he shucked away the idea of being a stay-at-home dad for the school year. Seriously, all it took was me saying, "Are you sure?" once and "Too bad there isn't a way for both of you to do research at the same time" the next day, and Dad looked at me like, well, like a buffalo looks at prairie grass. Before I knew it, he had pulled me into a rib-crunching hug and started talking about how maybe his dad could take us in for a few months; how I was such a trooper and how much I'd get a kick out of the old man. It wasn't like I agreed to it. I just sort of nodded and Mom congratulated me on being so mature while Dad spouted off buffalo facts.

So here we were, Mom and me, moving in with Gramps, who lived about forty-five minutes outside DC. Rather than rent an apartment like we'd planned, Mom and I were shacking up with Gramps for the next year.

And speaking of that school year, ironing out all the details for this new move-in-with-Gramps plan meant that I'd be starting classes two weeks after classes started for everyone else. So much for "normal."

I glared out my window at Gramps's house. Dad and Gramps aren't exactly close; this was the first time I was seeing his place. Picture a long, sprawling, bright yellow ranch-style home, with one wall red-bricked and a giant metal star embedded on it. That was my first clue that Gramps might have an odd sense of style. Second clue, and I'm not even joking here, was the yard horse.

"What is that?" I pointed to the cement horse standing in the middle of a circle of pansies. It was more of a pony, I guess, standing upright as if about to jump or neigh or whatever horses do when they rear up. The body was painted brown and eyes black. Whoever painted it wasn't light with the brush. The black eyes were drippy and scary looking.

Dad sighed. "It's our yard horse."

Mom and I stared at him until he continued. "Your grandma had a thing for horses. Always wanted a pony." He shrugged, like a cement yard horse was a normal thing. Like it was a natural conclusion when you want a pony but lived in the suburbs.

"Why is it wearing a sunhat?" I asked. Its little triangle ears popped out from a yellow bonnet tied under its chin. A matching little yellow apron hung down from its waist.

Dad huffed again. "When my mom was sick, Dad dressed it up for the seasons to make her laugh. Became a habit, I guess."

"Oh," I said, noticing the gardening tools hanging in the horse's apron pockets. "Because that's not bizarre or anything."

"Forget the horse, okay." Dad's voice boomed in the little car. "Clearly, Gramps could use the company."

"Why? He has a yard horse," I grumbled. I knew I was pushing it, but I felt this was one of those occasions where I was entitled to be a bit of a jerk. After all, I was about to move in with an old man who dressed up horses.

Dad waved his massive hand in the air like he was scattering my question. "He's looking forward to getting to know his only grandson."

If I could've rolled my eyes, I would've. He and Mom were totally playing Gramps and me. I heard him on the phone with Gramps a week or so ago, saying, "Ryder's going to need a steady figure at home." At the same time, he spouted off to me that the old man was the one who needed someone around.

"Can't I come with you?" I whined. "I could help you with your research."

"Now, Ryder," said Mom, her hand landing lightly on my shoulder, "for months you've been droning on about wanting to go to a regular school again. Here's your chance! And besides, the only way not to fall victim to swarms of Alaskan mosquitos is to not shower for a week at a time. It won't be pleasant."

I shuddered.

For a minute or two we sat in the car in silence, windows rolled down and sweat beading on my forehead. A high-pitched grunt to my right—my blind spot—made us turn our heads toward the sound. I had to shift entirely around to see what made the noise. If I had been at

Addison, I would've popped out my fake eye and rubbed it against my shirt to show how surprised I was by what I saw. Because there, on the front lawn beside Gramps's house, was a girl about my age. She held a huge stick-like thing, as tall as her and thinner than a broomstick. She whipped it around and stabbed it outward. The girl's chin-length hair swirled around her face as she twirled and jumped in the most incredible dance I had ever seen. But it wasn't a dance at all, I realized. It was like something out of a kung fu movie.

Dad whistled low. "At least we know the neighborhood's safe."

I slunk into the seat when Dad opened his car door. The girl stopped her routine and glanced over at us. *Maybe she didn't see me*, I thought, forgetting for a minute that, of course, she saw me. I mean, I was twisted around in the wrong direction, staring at her with my mouth hanging open. I am nothing if not smooth, right?

I lay across the back seat and groaned.

"Come on, buddy. It's just one year," coaxed Mom, mistakenly thinking my groan was about my entire life and not just the pretty girl next door.

My parents had offered to enroll me again at Addison, something I hadn't even told Alice. But I couldn't swallow the shame of heading back after the big send-off everyone gave me. So here we were, stuck with Gramps.

All I really remembered was his laugh, the way it sounded like a crow. *Cah, cah, cah.*

It echoed through me again just thinking about it. *Cah, cah, cah.*

Then I noticed Dad twisting his jaw around—a look usually reserved for me—and realized I was hearing Gramps's laugh for real.

"There he is," said Gramps, throwing open the back door to Mom's car and holding out a huge wrinkled hand. "My grandson! Let me get a look at you."

I grabbed his hand to shake and screamed as a jolt swept up my arm.

"*Cah, cah, cah!*" The crazy old man cackled. "Got you! I got you good!" He turned his hand to flash a round disc with buttons across the top. "The ol' electric hand-shake. Got you good."

I twisted my neck so fast to see if that girl was watching me and got the hot juice in my neck. You know, when you turn your head too quickly, something pops and *boom*! Hot juice trickles down the inside of your neck. Never happened to you? Lucky dog. Anyway, sure enough, there she was, arms crossed, leaning against that long staff and not even trying not to laugh.

I squinted at Gramps as he chuckled so hard he failed to notice no one else joined in. He was about my height, about five feet six inches. The little sprigs of hair he had

18

left were combed down across the top of his head. He had Dad's bushy eyebrows and brown-almost-black eyes and my skinny build. All I can say is, I guess Grams, may she rest in peace, must've been enormous, because Dad certainly didn't get his Hulk-like build from this guy.

Mom darted forward, dodging Gramps's out-stretched hand and kissed his wrinkled cheek. "Hi, Richie. It's nice to see you again."

Technically, my name is Richie, too. In fact, some-times Mom and Dad slip up and call me Richie, even though I've gone by my middle name of Ryder since sixth grade. (I mean, seriously, if you could go by Richie or Ryder, wouldn't you choose option B?) I know what you're thinking: Richie Ryder? Who the heck names their kid Richie Ryder? My parents. That's who. Richie Ryder Raymond. Say it three times fast. I dare you.

"So, Richie, we're going to be roomies, eh?" Gramps slipped the buzzer into his pocket.

"The boy prefers to be called Ryder now," Dad huffed as he pulled my enormous suitcase from the trunk.

"That so," Gramps replied. I didn't like the wink he shot my way.

"No, really," I said. "My name's Ryder."

"Yeah. 'Course it is," Gramps said, waving his hands like he was shooing away a fly. "No problem . . . Richie."

I thought I heard a tinkling laugh from next door but refused to look.

Dad slammed his huge hand on my shoulder, making me feel an inch shorter. "Bye, son."

Part of me wanted to turn away from him, to load him down with guilt for leaving. But he looked so sad. I couldn't do it.

"See you, Dad. Hope the buffalo are real . . . I don't know. Whatever buffalo are supposed to be."

Dad's eyes welled up. "Thanks, Ryder," he said and turned to Mom, wiping at his eyes.

And just because this particular moment couldn't get any worse, that's when Mom and Dad locked in a passionate embrace.

"Goodbye, my darling," Dad boomed.

"I will miss you tremendously," Mom cried. Dad pulled her against him as she sobbed into his massive chest.

I know, I know. Parents who love each other are a blessing, right? A good thing. But while Mom and Dad were certainly used to leaving me behind—ahem, at boarding school for the past two years—they were totally out of practice on being without each other.

If I wanted to know what my disgusted oh-geez-now-they're-kissing face looked like, all I had to do was glance at Gramps.

"That's just wrong," he muttered. He slapped his hand on my shoulder and turned me away. "This is one of those times when you should be grateful you only have one eye, Richie."

"It's Ryder," I snapped. "And I don't think we're at the point in our relationship where you can make one-eye jokes." And here was the thing: I wasn't even kidding. Just who did this guy think he was?

"*Cah, cah, cah!*" Gramps held his rolling stomach with his other hand. "Good one, kid. Good one."

Not able to take another second of listening to Mom and Dad smooching or Gramps crowing, I grabbed my bag and threw open the front door to what would be home for the next year.

Then I quickly walked back outside, rubbed my eyes, and tried again. Clearly, Gramps's front door was a portal to another dimension, one set in the 1970s. That's the only explanation for what I saw before me.

Everything—and I mean *everything*—in Gramps's house was straight out of the 1970s. Not familiar with the '70s? You are *so* lucky. Here's a run-down for you, from the ground up: vinyl paisley swirled linoleum flooring in olive green and gold, except for the orange shag carpeting in the living room. More orange on the wood-paneled walls.

I forced my feet to take more steps inside and fell onto a mustard yellow couch to take it all in. Rock hard. You'd think by now it'd at least be broken in. The nubby fabric made the underside of my sweaty knees itch. The coffee and end tables looked like huge pieces of wood dipped in about a thousand coats of clear nail polish. I think it's called lacquer. All of this was jazzed up with mirrored panels inlaid on about every wall.

I heard the screen door swing open behind me and the sharp intake of Mom's breath.

"Home, sweet home!" Gramps clapped his hands together.

I twisted to see Mom's face. Her eyes were bugging out as she looked around the room. "We had planned to keep most of our furnishings in storage," she finally whispered. "But maybe we could bring some here. You know, update things a bit."

"Nah," Gramps said. "Ain't broke, don't fix it." He sat next to me, his arms extending out over the stiff top of the couch. "These are classic lines. Built to last. Can you believe this living room set has held up since Marlene decorated back before your father was born?" he asked me.

I numbly nodded. "I can believe it."

I heard the ping of a text and grabbed my phone from my pocket. Gramps was sitting to the left of me so I sort of had to elbow him a little to read it.

"The lady friend already checking on you?" Gramps elbowed me back. I shuddered on the inside a little, realizing he thought I had been nudging him so he could see the text. It was from Alice.

How is it going?

I turned my body so my back was to Gramps.

My gramps is a disco-era-loving freak.

The ping from Alice's return text sounded in seconds. One of the benefits of Addison School for the Blind: despite her eyes, Alice was now plugged in like the rest of our generation, using an app that let her hear both incoming messages and her own keystrokes as she types replies.

Can't be so bad. You must've just gotten there.

I quickly typed back.

Remember when we went for that road trip with James and Sarah to the nature reserve and Tooter ate all the beef jerky from our backpack?

Alice pinged back a *y* for yes.

Remember how it started pouring. We had to put the windows up?

Another *y*.

And then Tooter started farting?

Small pause.

OMG.

And then he got diarrhea?

Uh-oh.

I sighed as I typed.

Yep. That's how bad my life stinks right now.

Mom hoisted her suitcase into the guest room across from the living room. "I hear all those messages coming in, Ryder. You better connect to the Wi-Fi before you use up all your data for the month."

And that's when things went from bad to worse. Because there were no Wi-Fi options. "Gramps," I asked in a shaky voice, "what's your Wi-Fi network? I can't find it on my phone."

"Network? We get at least four networks on the television. All you need is right there." He pointed to the gigantic box television set in the middle of the room. I had missed it at first, thinking it was a giant dresser. But, nope. It was a television.

I swallowed down the panic rising in my chest. "For the Internet, I mean. How do you get online?"

"*Pshcaw!*" Gramps waved his hands like he was shooing a bug. "Only time I go online is senior citizen free donut day at the Stop N Shop Grocery. Lines like you wouldn't believe."

Mom was suddenly beside me, her face pale and eyes wide. "You don't have Internet access in your home?" she hissed.

"No need," Gramps said in an if-it-ain't-broke-don't-fix-it voice.

Mom sank into the couch on the other side of me with a thud. "How am I going to do my research from home?"

"How am I going to stay in touch with my friends?" I shook my head. Could this be possible? Could there really be people who aren't online at all? I forgot to blink and Artie got a little wobbly in my socket. (By the way, that's my artificial eye's name. Artie. Like, *arti*ficial eye.) I rubbed it back into place.

Mom slapped her hands on her thighs. "Well, I'll call the cable company right now. See if we can upgrade."

"Don't have cable either," Gramps piped up.

I felt all the bones leave my body as I crumpled farther into the nubby couch.

"Then I'll arrange for that as well," Mom said. Her usual buzzing soft tone was gone. She sounded a lot like Dad, actually, all gruff and serious. She was on the phone with the cable company in less than a minute. She did this thing when she was on the phone where she flitted around the house, moving from room to room like a moth trapped behind a window. I doubt she even realized she did it.

While she paced around, I turned back to Gramps. "So, if you don't have cable and you don't have the Internet, what do you do all day?"

"Oh, you know, spend time with the General." Gramps pushed out his bottom lip and nodded like what he said made any more sense than not having Wi-Fi in the twenty-first century.

"Who is the General?" Maybe this general was one of Gramps's old-fart friends. I shifted on the couch, trying to find a comfortable spot. I stretched out my legs and crossed my ankles on the lacquered coffee table.

And was suddenly and viciously attacked!

A hissing ball of yellow darted out from under the couch and sank its teeth into that soft spot above my ankle. I think it's called the Achilles tendon.

"That's the General," Gramps chuckled. He pulled the still-hissing-also-howling beast away, but not before it raked my leg with its claws. "Richie, meet General MacCathur the Second." He held up one of the cat's paws in a wave. Its claws were still extended.

"Seriously?" I yelped.

The cat spit at me, its yellow eyes narrowed.

"What was General MacCathur the First like?" I asked.

"Oh, he was mean as the devil," Gramps said. "General MacCathur the Second? She is much gentler."

Chapter Three

"What's the best kind of pet, Richie?" Gramps asked the morning of my first day of school.

"A dead cat," I muttered.

"That's right," he said, having misheard me. "A kitty cat. They're perfect. Get it? *Purr*-fect."

At that moment, we were both looking at my new black backpack, which I had carefully stocked with eight notebooks—all black—a lunchbox—also black—and various pens, erasers, and flash drives. You guessed it, all were black. I was going to be the new guy, a man of mystery, right? Hence the black.

And, yeah, maybe buying only black things was a sort of silent protest. I don't just mean because of the whole moving in with Gramps thing. More a protest against Gramps's sense of style, or lack of style, that is.

The only thing of this decade in the house was the huge new TV set Mom installed in front of Gramps's

rust-colored recliner, the lines of cable wire running down to the basement, a new router, and, unfortunately, General MacCathur the Second.

Between the devil cat and the dark, horrid colors, dim lighting, and mirrors, my one eye was working overdrive. Even having been here for a few days, I was still getting used to the rooMs. They all looked way bigger than they were, thanks to the huge mirrors hanging everywhere. I even walked straight into one on the way to the kitchen for breakfast! Gramps, of course, thought this was hysterical. Time-warped geezer laughed so hard I thought he was choking at first.

I think General MacCathur laughed, too. I seriously doubt you can really even call the hideous beast a cat. That's like a major insult to the cat species, I'm sure. Because this was more like a yellow-eyed demon. General MacCathur loved to curl through my feet as I walked—always sticking to the right, where I couldn't spot her until too late—so *bam*! I'd fall to the shag carpeting. I quickly figured out her second favorite form of torment. General MacCathur tucked under the second to last step on Gramps's stairway. Just as my foot was about to make contact with the last step, I'd hear the horrid hiss and feel the prick of her pointy devil teeth in the same soft spot above my ankle she'd attacked on day one of being here.

And now we had this. General MacCathur the Second curled up in the middle of my backpack, furring all of it with her bushy yellow hair.

You can imagine how I felt seeing that my all-black-all-the-time gear had some added shag carpeting of its own, thanks to the demon cat. Awesome.

I reached toward the bag, hoping to send the cat flying. Don't get me wrong: I love animals. I once spent an entire afternoon carrying around Tooter, Alice's oldie moldy dog, and it was awesome (toxic farts aside). General MacCathur would probably eat Tooter for breakfast. She hissed and raked her claws across my arm like she could hear my thoughts.

"Ow!" I howled. "Move it, fleabag!"

General MacCathur blinked huge yellow eyes at me and raised a leg to lick her butt.

"Now, now, Ryder," said Mom, floating by without moving her eyes from the lines of the research paper she was editing. She swooped General MacCathur into her arMs. The demented beast purred even as it glared at me. "You've just got to show her some kindness. Respect her boundaries."

"Respect her boundaries? She was in *my* backpack!" I guess I couldn't be too surprised. Spend your day surrounded by insects and you can't be easily annoyed, even by a twenty-pound cat determined to ruin your day.

"Next time, I'll just zip her up in there. Give you a nice surprise 'bout lunchtime," Gramps laughed.

"Whatever." I brushed the fur off the backpack as best I could with the side of my hand. A whiff of the General's musky stench hit my nose as I zipped shut the bag. "See you later, Mom!" I called and headed for the door.

"Ryder, wait!" I could hear Mom rushing toward me. "Ryder!"

"Mom, I'm going to miss the bus," I called.

"Stop!" Mom ordered in her don't-mess-with-me tone. I stopped.

"I don't think it's a good idea for you to take the bus," she said. Her beady eyes flicked back and forth across my face.

"Why?" I snapped. I could hear the rumble of the bus as it wheezed down the road.

"It's your first day," Mom said.

"Everyone else started two weeks ago, Mom. It's not that big of a deal."

"Yes, but it's your first day in the school district," Mom said. "I'd just feel better if you had someone there to walk you in and everything."

"Mom!" I whined. "I'm in eighth grade! I can't have my mommy walking me into the office!"

"*Cah, cah, cah!*" I whipped around to see Gramps pulling on leather driving gloves just behind me. He grinned around the keys, which were in his mouth. Swiping them from his lips, he said, "Don't worry, Richie. Mommy's heading to work. I'll make sure you look groovy in front of your friends. Let's boogie!"

"Don't do this to me, Mom," I begged.

"I just need to make sure the administration remembers your accommodations, that's all, Ryder."

"*I* can tell them!" By accommodations, Mom meant that I had to sit in the front, toward the right side of the room so I could see more easily with my left eye. Stuff like that. No biggie, nothing I couldn't handle.

In a lowered voice, Mom added, "Gramps offered to do this for you. It's a rare and wonderful thing when he's willing to leave the house these days, so please, just let him."

"Mom, he's wearing white pants. Tight white pants."

She sighed. "I think it's not just his house that hasn't been updated in the past forty years. His wardrobe, too. It's sort of interesting, really. That he's been stuck in this time period since Marlene passed away. Kind of reminds me of *Jurassic Park*—he's like the mosquito stuck in amber for centuries."

Mom's eyes get this faraway look whenever she thinks of the dinosaur movie. Seeing the original movie when she was a teenager made her get on the whole entomologist bandwagon, though she thankfully isn't interested

31

in resurrecting dinosaurs. Just interested, apparently, in forcing me to kick off day one in public middle school accompanied by one.

"I can't believe you're doing this to me."

A horn honked in the driveway and Mom pushed me toward the door.

"Calm down, Ryder. He means well." Mom kissed my cheek. "Good luck today!"

Do you know what an Oldsmobile Cutlass is? It's a giant, stretched-out car that, if it's driven by my gramps, belches out bursts of grayish black smoke. His was a sparkly gold color and had windows that you actually had to crank down. I know this because that's just what he was doing as he lay on the horn yet again, even though I stood right there by the front door. Hanging his head out the window, he yelled, "Whad'ya think, Richie? Ready to pick up some chicks?"

That, of course, was the moment the gorgeous girl from the day before left her house to get onto the bus, which, of course, had every window open so that everyone inside saw Gramps, heard Gramps, and now—cherry on top—could watch him wiggle in his seat to the disco tunes blaring from his open windows. What was the sound? Was that someone singing the words, "Jive Talkin'"? And was Gramps belting along in a squeaky falsetto?

Yes. Yes, he was.

I didn't want to, I really didn't, but I twisted my head to see if the gorgeous girl was watching. And, since the bus was to the right, that meant there was no sly is-she-or-isn't-she glance. Nope, I had to totally commit. Sort of like how Gramps had totally committed to getting down with his bad self.

Yes. Yes, she was.

And also laughing.

Awesome.

Gramps didn't just pull up to the school building and let me out. Nope, he walked me into Papuaville Middle School. I rammed my hands in my pockets and prayed for an asteroid to fall on my head.

"I seriously can figure out where to go on my own," I told Gramps.

Gramps's eyes raked me up and down. "Look at you there with your plain old jeans and T-shirt, walking in here swiveling your head all around like a doofus. What you need is some confidence. You should strut." He jerked his chin out, did this odd flapping thing with his arms, and shimmied his butt as he walked. Picture a chicken crossed with a cow, in the skin of an old, flabby man wearing white pants. Yep, that's exactly what he looked like.

"You realize that 'swiveling my head all around like a doofus' is the only way I can see what's going on, right?" I snapped.

"Yeah, you should stop doing that." Gramps yanked open the door to the school office.

"Wait a sec," I said, grabbing Gramps's polyester sleeve. I leaned in to study the picture of the school mascot to make sure my eye wasn't deceiving me. "Papuaville Middle School's mascots . . . are those wombats?"

"Wombats?" Gramps scoffed. "Why in the world would they be wombats? Those," he said, pointing to two flat-headed, buck-toothed, potato-shaped mascots, "are guinea pigs."

"We're the Guinea Pigs? The Papuaville Guinea Pigs?"

"The Papuaville *Fighting* Guinea Pigs." Gramps threw open the door farther and called out to the cluster of secretaries, "Hey, ladies!"

I let the door drift shut in front of me. I'm not sure if my one remaining eye could withstand the sight of Gramps flirting with the school secretaries.

"You okay?"

I turned to find none other than gorgeous girl next door standing right in front of me. I worked on getting my jaw to close. She was even prettier up close. The fluorescent lights made her dark brown hair shinier, her light brown eyes brighter. Her mouth twitched a little as I stared.

Too late, I realized she had been watching my eyes while I stared at her. Now her eyes flicked back and forth, trying to figure out which eye to stick with. My artificial eye, it does move. It just doesn't *quite* keep up with the other eye. In fact, if you saw me randomly you wouldn't be like, "Oh, look. That guy has something wrong with his eye." Nope, that realization would come later once you were standing just a few feet away from me and watching my face, the way Beautiful Neighbor girl was now. She totally saw the *not quite* part of my eye movement.

I could work with this. Not to brag, but I've become a bit of an expert at monopolizing people's uncertainties when it comes to my eyes. I gave her my swaggiest half-smile, half-nod look. "Hey, I've been keeping an eye out for you."

She sucked in her breath but didn't take the bait. "Um, I'm Jocelyn."

"Ryder." I grinned at her, watching the edges of her mouth pause before smiling back. "You live next door to my gramps, right?" Both of us paused as Gramps's *cah, cah, cah* laugh boomed from inside the office.

"Yeah, he's great."

"Obviously you don't know him very well."

Jocelyn smiled, but whatever else she was going to say was cut off by the bell. "See you later, Ryder. Maybe we'll have a class together."

"Yeah, I'll *see* you." The words tasted lame even as they slipped out of my mouth. For some reason, I stretched *see* into something long and heavy, and it fell like a thud. The only thing worse than a bad joke is nothing. Nothing is worse than a bad joke.

Ugh. Even *that* was a bad joke.

I texted Alice, even though I knew I could be getting her in trouble with the teachers at Addison if she was caught with her phone in class.

Crisis. Cute girl doesn't think I'm funny.

Gramps left the office, waving a piece of paper in his fist. Behind him, I could see the secretaries settle back in their seats, shaking their heads. For a second, I felt bad for the old man. He thought he was making jokes all the time, when really, *he* was the joke.

"Got your schedule, Richie Ryder." Gramps's idea of compromise was to call me both of my names. "Took a guess about the experiential classes—the ones you can sign up for as an elective."

"What? There are optional classes? What are they?" I asked.

"Oh, you know, wood shop. Music. Art. Theater. Things like that."

36

"But which one—"

The bell rang again. "You better get to class. You've got homeroom with Miss Singer on the second floor to start." Gramps shoved the paper into my hand, turned me around, and pushed my body toward the stairway.

I heard the soft *cah, cah, cah* of his laugh as I trudged up the stairs.

Chapter Four

Homeroom was on the right of the hallway at the top of the stairs, which meant zeroing in on the room number took some concentration. Here's the deal: I could turn my head pretty far around but I suddenly became aware of everyone watching me in the halls. So I was suave about it, stopping to tie my shoes when I got close to a doorway, shifting on my heels a little while I was stooped, then standing to see that the door number was *bam!* Right in front of me. This one was room 210, and my class was 206. I meandered down another few doors then—imagine that! My shoe was untied again. I positioned myself, quickly tied my already-tied sneaker, and stood to confirm. Yep. Room 206. Like I said, suave.

I guess I was too busy being self-congratulatory to notice the love of my life was standing beside me. I ran right into Jocelyn and she fell backward a few steps and into the boy behind her.

"Hey!" the guy barked. "Watch where you're going."

"It's fine," said Jocelyn, her cheeks turning pink. "I don't think he saw me."

"Of course he saw you," the guy said. He put his arm around Jocelyn, like I might barrel into her again. "He turned right into you."

"No, man, I didn't see her," I started to explain.

The guy jerked his chin at me. What did that mean? Was it like he was backward nodding, pushing his face up instead of down? Or was it some primitive challenge? He stood there, hand on Jocelyn's shoulder, pushing-but-not-quite-pushing her toward the door and away from me. But his body was facing me square on. He had brilliant green eyes and the longest lashes I'd ever seen on a boy. I know what you're thinking: that's an odd thing for a guy to notice about another guy. But it's true. They were so long they looked kind of tangled.

And here's the thing: I have this condition. Alice diagnosed me once, as she claims to suffer from the same ailment. I could hear her voice in my head as I thought of it. *When you're nervous, you just blurt whatever you're thinking, like you can't hold the words in another second. Like diarrhea of the mouth.* So there you have it. Diarrhea of the mouth struck me, and I blurted, "Do you have to brush your eyelashes? Because they are mega, mega long."

"What?" This time the guy jerked backward.

Jocelyn's cough into her shoulder sounded an awful lot like a laugh.

My stupid mouth stretched into a grin at the sound of it. "Sorry, it's just, I've never seen such lashes. Do the mascara people know about you? 'Cause you should be in commercials—"

Lash Boy dropped his arm and did this move where he stepped super close to me, pushing his chest out. I'd seen gorillas do that once in a documentary Dad was watching. It's a show of dominance, I think. If I were a monkey, I was supposed to cower or throw my poop or something. But I am not a monkey and I was already pressed up against wall. So I did something really stupid. I leaned back toward *him*. "Yep. Thanks to how you're standing, I can tell for sure. Definitely the longest lashes I've ever seen. Not that I've seen many this close."

By now, I became aware that about a half-dozen other kids were gathered around us. "Have you guys seen his lashes?" I said to them. "They're like the lashes on doll babies. You know the ones that blink open and shut?" Sure enough, Lash Boy slowly blinked at me.

"You're a freak!" Lash Boy hissed as everyone around us laughed. "What the heck is wrong with you?"

A hand clamped down on my shoulder and Lash Boy's at the same time. Oh, great. Perfect way to meet my homeroom teacher. The woman looked a bit like

41

a potato. I think most of the time she must've looked like a super nice, teachery teacher. But right then, she was a boiling hot mad potato teacher. "Mr. Waters!" she screamed at Lash Boy. "I am embarrassed and ashamed of how you would treat a differently abled new student! Your parents are going to be crushed when I call them this evening!"

"Wait, wait, wait!" I stammered as Lash Boy's face turned a frightening shade of purple. His mouth flopped open and shut a couple times, making him look even more like a doll. "He wasn't talking about my—"

At the same time, Lash Boy repeated, "Differently abled?"

"I admire you standing up for Max," Miss Singer said, "but I refuse to ignore such a blatant example of bullying." She clapped her hands together three times. "Everyone! In the classroom. Time for class." On cue, the bell rang.

"You!" She pointed into Lash Boy's, aka Max's, chest. "You get to wherever you need to be. Just know that I *will* be notifying your parents about what I just witnessed." Miss Singer pushed past us both.

"It wasn't like that!" Max gasped. His face drained from cherry red to white in seconds, like watching strawberry syrup sink to the bottom of a glass of milk. "I didn't mean . . ."

I sighed. "Look, I'll make it right," I said to him. But then, of course, I opened my mouth again as he started to look relieved. "Do you accept payment in the form of mascara or do you have a different sort of currency in mind?" I swear, if I could rein in my wit, I would. But my verbal brilliance cannot be restrained, even when faced with someone who very clearly couldn't keep up. Lash Boy's mouth flapped open and shut a couple times.

"Let it go," Jocelyn whispered to him. She turned Max's body and gave him a half push in the opposite direction. "Just get to class."

After a moment of Max just staring over his shoulder at me with the same scary purple face, I realized that he only partly was looking at me with hatred. The other part was still trying to figure out what Miss Singer meant by differently abled. And seriously, I'm a nice guy. I couldn't let Lash Boy burn. Plus, the look Jocelyn pinned me with—sharp and waiting—made me move. And truth be told, he hadn't called me a freak because of Artie.

Lash Boy called me a freak because of . . . well . . . *me*. I shook my head and rushed after Miss Singer, who had settled in behind her desk and was scribbling into the notebook. As I approached, she closed it with a quick slap.

"Listen, Miss Singer," I said. "I know I should intro-duce myself and all, but it seems you already know all about me. I just need you to know: Max wasn't calling me a freak because of my eye. I swear, I sort of provoked him, and—"

"What's wrong with your eye?" A kid who had been hanging around the teacher's desk now leaned in and stared at my face.

Miss Singer sighed, folding her hands under her chin. "I see we've just got to deal with this plainly, Richie Ryder."

"It's just Ryder," I interrupted.

"That's odd," she murmured. "It says here specifically that you wish to be called Richie Ryder at all times." She squinted her eyes at the computer screen, where I guess she was reading about me. "Your grandfather was very clear about this to the office personnel."

"Gramps!" I growled. "Please just call me Ryder."

"Fine." Miss Singer stood and put her hands on her round hips. "This is a small town. Most of these kids have known each other since kindergarten. And this group in particular is close. We middle school teachers looped with them, so they had us for all of their courses in seventh grade, too. You're going to stand out, for a few reasons." She squinted at me, eyes drifting from my fire-red hair, one eye, and freckles, then to my too-tall, too-skinny frame to my too-long feet. "Let's get this over with, shall we, Ryder? I find it's best to face issues head on. At Papuaville, homeroom classes stay for first period. That means once I take attendance and we're officially into biology class, we'll address the issue with the class."

"What issue?" I asked, as all around us kids settled into their seats. Miss Singer motioned for me to stay put in front of the room.

"Don't worry," Jocelyn whispered as she settled into the seat in front of me. "Miss Singer means well. It's just that she used to be a kindergarten teacher."

"Oh," I said, too shocked that Jocelyn was actually speaking to me to think of anything clever to say. (*Oh.* It's not even a word. It's just a letter with another pity letter tacked on, trying to make a noise into a real word.) I sat down in the seat to the right of her.

"Um, that's my seat." A tall kid with floppy brown hair and ruddy face pointed to the chair I was sitting in. His voice was surprisingly deep, like a frog croaking, considering his skinny body.

"Oh, sorry." But I was slow to stand, not wanting to move away from Jocelyn. I thought about Alice, how she had admitted that the only reason she really sought me out at first was because I was easy to spot with my red hair. Maybe I just wanted to be around Jocelyn because she was the only person here who had actually seemed friendly. But just then I took a deep breath, ready to sigh and move away. When I did, I breathed in the soft powdery flower smell of her hair. Nope. Not just because she was nice. Because I was hard-core crushing on this girl.

Apparently so was floppy-haired-seat-reclaimer. "I sit next to Jocelyn," he said, a little louder. Two panicky red blotches appeared on his cheeks. Guess I wasn't vacating the seat fast enough.

"Logan!" Miss Singer snapped from across the room. "I'm giving our new student that seat. You can sit here now." She pointed to an empty seat in the back of the room. It was next to a chubby girl with greasy hair who was actively digging in her ears. I shuddered as she took off her glasses and used the arm of it to reach farther into the ear canal. She sucked the glob of wax off the tip.

Logan must've been watching, too, because when I turned back around those two splotches on his face had bled into a full-fired face of fury. He shook his head at me and stomped off to the back of the room. Great. Add Logan to the growing list of people who hated me—and I'd only been in school for just under an hour.

Jocelyn laughed beside me like she could hear my thoughts.

"What?" I asked.

She shook her head, still laughing. "It's just—you sure do make new friends fast, huh?"

I laughed back. "How long have you lived next door to Gramps?"

"All my life. He's awesome, isn't he?"

"Gramps? You and I have different definitions of awesome."

"Oh, come on!" Jocelyn leaned forward, resting her hands under her chin. She pulled the sleeves of her shirt down so they were stretched up to her knuckles. Her dark hair swung forward, covering the rest of her hands. "Mr. Raymond's the best. He's the only person who gives out full-sized candy bars on Halloween. I didn't trick-or-treat one year . . . I didn't want to . . ." Jocelyn twisted the ends of her shirt sleeves in her hands. "But your grandpa, he knew how much I loved candy. So he came over in costume and hand-delivered it to my house."

"My gramps? Wait—he wasn't dressed up like a pony, was he?"

Jocelyn grinned. "No, he was a duck. I think he called himself Disco Duck, but I'm pretty sure it was a Donald Duck costume. He has a spot-on Donald voice, too."

I leaned back in the chair, crossing my arms over my chest. A memory tugged at me, a dream of a duck talking to me in the hospital after my surgery.

"Huh," I said. "That surprises me. I would've thought he'd be all over the trick part of trick-or-treat."

"Oh, he was!" A smile tugged at her lips. "He made me pull his finger first."

"No way." I shook my head. "That's wrong." Gramps had gotten me to pull his finger exactly once. I think I was three. I tugged on his finger and *bam!* Gross grandpa fart erupted out of him.

Jocelyn laughed behind her fingers. "He gave me the Fartinator, too."

"The what?"

"The Fartinator," she said. "You know, a little remote control with buttons for different fart sounds. And I got a full-sized candy bar."

I was pretty sure I had gotten the full force of a genuine Gramps release when I was three. "Doesn't sound like much of a joke, really," I said. "Kind of lame."

Jocelyn shrugged and opened a notebook as Miss Singer called out for the class to quiet. Homeroom, which was really just a quick attendance, slid right into biology class with all the same students after the bell. I was relieved I wouldn't have to search for another classroom. That is, until Miss Singer nodded to me in a we'll-address-you-soon sort of way.

"I think your gramps is funny," Jocelyn said during the break. "The Fartinator made me laugh so hard I cried." She pressed her lips together, like she was tasting a thought another few seconds before speaking. I noticed that she pulled on the edges of her sleeves—already pulled down to her fingers—until her hands all but disappeared inside of them. Even quieter than before, she breathed, "It's nice to just laugh, even if it is at something as stupid as a Fartinator. Everyone around me is always so serious, so careful with me."

The room quieted down as other kids followed suit and pulled out notebooks and pencils. I knew I shouldn't—I mean, she made it pretty clear that the conversation was over by hunching over her notebook. And Lash Boy made it crystal clear that I should back off getting to know Jocelyn. But I couldn't resist leaning into the gap between our desks. She looked so sad suddenly. I thought maybe she wished she had swallowed that last sentence she spoke instead.

"You know," I whispered, "I'm pretty funny, too."

"Oh, yeah?" Jocelyn didn't look up from her notes but she did tilt her chin a little in my direction.

"I bet I can make you laugh."

Jocelyn shrugged.

I jumped as Miss Singer's hand landed on my shoulder. She motioned for me to stand. "All right, class," she boomed. "We have a new student."

"Ryder!" I cut in before she could introduce me as Richie Ryder.

Miss Singer put her arm around my shoulder and squeezed. Her eyes were wide and blinking, and she pressed her lips together. Giving my shoulder another awkward squeeze, she turned to the class. "Now, friends," she said, "I'd like you all to welcome Rich—I mean, *Ryder*—to our class."

She looked at the class as though she really thought they'd all chant *welcome*. From the way Miss Singer's potato face crumpled inward, I think she really was missing teaching kindergarteners.

In the same drawn-out, let's-share-our-feelings voice, my teacher continued, "Ryder is here from a school in South Carolina called Addison School for the Blind." Slight pause to acknowledge the whiplash effect of her words—kids suddenly straightened up in their seats, squinting as they stared at my heated face.

Someone said, "What the—?"

Miss Singer raised the hand not wrapped around me. "Being a new student is tough, isn't it?" she crooned. "It's even harder when you're differently abled. Let's all put on our compassion hats"—I swear, she actually mimed putting on an invisible hat—"and give our warmest welcome to Richie Ryder."

"It's just Ryder," I mumbled.

"Any questions or comments?" Miss Singer continued.

This was it. I could just stand there like the doofus Gramps set me up to be, stared at like one of Mom's bugs, lobbed questions I didn't feel like answering. Or, I could stop this right now, Ryder style. Jocelyn raised an eyebrow like she had heard my internal debate.

I raised my hand.

Miss Singer's little eyes popped. "No, sweetie," she said slowly. "The questions are for the class about *you*."

"I have a question for the class, though," I replied. I took a deep breath and nodded to myself like I was really considering sharing something deep. I let my eye sweep across the room, knowing everyone's gaze would snag on Artie. Then I asked, "What did the one-eyed pirate say to the captain?"

"Excuse me?"

"Eye, Captain." No one moved. Jocelyn's eyes widened, but no one laughed. "Instead of Aye-aye? Get it?" Someone in the back groaned. "All right, not my finest. What did the cavemen call the one-eyed dinosaur?" Now a couple people grinned. "DoYouThinkItSawUs." A laugh erupted out of the girl with the ear wax, so hard it sounded like she was choking. Or maybe she actually was choking. I took it as encouragement.

I rocked on my heels, firing out another one before Miss Singer could turn her potatoey grunts into words. "Where should the five-hundred-pound one-eyed monster go?"

"Where?" Jocelyn called out softly.

51

"On a diet." A few people kind of laughed. I took off my glasses and wiped at one of the lenses with the edge of my shirt. I cupped them in my hand, getting ready for the grand finale.

Miss Singer, voice stern, said, "I don't think this is appropriate—"

I cut her off, determined to reach the big finish. "Right, right, of course. It's been super inappropriate. Here's the deal: I have low vision in my left eye, about twenty-seventy acuity instead of twenty-twenty like the rest of you. And my right eye is plastic. I think what Miss Singer hoped to say was that it'd be great if you all "—pause while I brought my fingers up to Artie—" kept an eye out for me." And *pop*! I held my eye in my hand over my head.

A few kids laughed. One even hooted. But most kind of groaned. Sadly, Jocelyn was not among the laughers. She smiled and shook her head. "I thought it'd be round," she said.

I laughed. "Yeah," I said, flipping it around in my hands. "Most people think that." Actually it's kind of like a super thick, super big contact lens. Sort of oblong and flattish. I heard a couple more *huhs* but no laughs. Tough crowd, I guess.

I was a little surprised when a second later, as I was popping my eye back into place, everyone started buzzing. Suddenly Jocelyn rushed toward me, arms out. I stupidly raised mine, too. Like maybe she finally thought everything I had said was hilarious and was literally throwing herself at me. But she wasn't. She was throwing herself toward Miss Singer, beside me, who tumbled forward, out cold.

Yep. I made my biology teacher pass out.

"Wow," said the kid whose seat I had stolen. "She didn't even squirm when we had to dissect the frogs last year."

"Yeah," someone else said, "or the fetal pigs."

"Oh man," I muttered. Killing the teacher was not the way to impress girls and make friends. I shimmied my way in so that I could make sure Miss Singer was breathing. Her eyes moved back and forth behind closed lids. "I think she's waking!"

Slowly Miss Singer's eyes opened. And there I was, smack dab in front of her, staring at her with a lifeless eye. "*Aaargh*," she groaned, and passed out again.

Awesome.

Chapter Five

K now what's even worse than making your bio teacher pass out on your first day?

Having your crazy-pants grandpa pick your electives.

After homeroom and bio, I couldn't quite make out the abbreviation on my schedule for my next class. The letters were QLT and the room number started with a zero, meaning it was in the basement.

QLT? What could that possibly stand for?

I trudged down the stairs, getting plowed over by about fifty kids, still trying to figure out which class I was heading to. The whole eighth grade had electives for second period. I saw some poor fool dash by in a swimming suit and goggles. Another kid was toting an enormous canvas painting up the stairs. Everyone seemed in a super hurry to get where they were going. And weirdly, every single one of them was going up the stairs. I was the lone guppy going downstream in a river of salmon heading up.

"Oh, come on!" I yelled as yet again I was pushed into the railing.

"Wrong way!" someone snapped as she literally tried to walk through me. I pressed against the wall. Hate to say it, but man, I missed Addison. Everyone was so laid back there. Hallways were for casual conversations. For fist-bumping your buddy and making plans to catch up at lunch. Not this determined mosh pit. And let's just say it, there is a serious dearth of proper deodorizing going on among our age group. Seriously, ten quick swipes per pit, people. It's not that tough.

"Well, I have to go down! Not everyone can go up all the time!" I yelled back over my shoulder at the girl who had tried to pass straight through me.

When I turned back around, there was yet another person directly in front of me. I put my hands up to push this person back and at the exact same moment, for some reason I still don't get, I knew—just *knew*—what QLT stood for.

Quantum Leap Theory.

That had to be it. Gramps was a genius.

Here's a little trip down memory lane. Don't forget that in this moment, I'm trapped, spine squashed against the railing in a torrent of smelly middle-schoolers, but the mind is a magnificent thing capable of, in one second, reflecting on an entire memory. That's just what happened in that second. I was flooded with a memory. It was back when I was seven, right after I had been diagnosed. I remember that Mom and Dad cried a lot, but I wasn't really all that nervous. I mean, the doctors told us that my one eye had to be removed, but I still had the other one. Plus, I couldn't see much out of that bad eye anyway, so it didn't seem like a huge deal. Not for me, anyway. Mom and Dad on the other hand . . . Mom kept taking pictures of me. The tumors behind the eye made it look white in the flash, so she kept erasing the digital image and snapping another. "I just want one normal picture," she said. I don't know why I remember that so clearly, except that Mom sort of freaked out a little after saying it. Her face looked like paper, all crumpled up into itself.

She left the hospital room and it was just me and Gramps. I didn't know him super well, so I sort of jumped back when he dumped the bag he had been carrying around on the bed. It was a little travel movie player and a DVD. "It's the complete first season of *Quantum Leap*," he said, as though I had asked.

"Huh?" I said and picked up the DVD. There was a picture of a dorky man in a shiny leather jacket with, like, flames or lasers or something surrounding him.

Gramps sighed, grabbed the DVD, and put it into the player. The chair screeched as he yanked it over to settle next to my bed. "Richie, I'm going to tell you the honest truth. They're going to cut out your eye."

"I know," I said, but I remember being shocked a bit at the word "cut." I mean, I had guessed that much already but Mom and Dad kept using the word "remove" instead of cut. The doctors called it "the procedure."

"And there are a couple tumors behind your other eye."

I nodded. Most kids who have the type of cancer I did—retinoblastoma—only have it in one eye. If they're unlucky enough to have it in both eyes, most of the time that's because it's hereditary—something that runs in their family. Me? I'm unlucky *and* odd. I have no hereditary reason for having retinoblastoma but I somehow managed to have it in both eyes. The good news was that a type of radiation, or sort of laser-like treatment, killed the tumors behind my left eye. But the right eye had to go. More good news was that since it wasn't hereditary, it probably wouldn't ever come back. I was supposed to get scanned for it every year, just in case, though. (A part of my magnificent mind paused mid-memory and took note that I was due for one of those checkups.)

Anyway, Gramps still wasn't telling me anything new.

"Well, if those know-it-all docs weren't able to get rid of those tumors like they thought and you're already getting one eye yanked, we've got a limited amount of time to show you all the things you need to know. Things like how to be a man." He pressed play on the movie player.

"This show's going to tell me how to be a man?" I asked.

"Of course not. *Cah, cah, cah.* A lifetime of perfect vision wouldn't show you that. Being in the hospital, awaiting your surgery, that's no time for such an undertaking."

Gramps rooted around in his pockets, pulling out candy bars and sweets. "Richie, this is a ridiculous series about a man who ends up in a different body all the time, sailing through time and space. It's probably the stupidest premise that ever was. But it was big in the late eighties and now it's on sale on at Walmart in the five-ninety-nine bin."

"Why are we watching it, then?" I remember asking.

"It's that or sit here, thinking about how you're down one, maybe two eyes."

"Oh."

Gramps handed me some red licorice when I started to cry. "*That's* being a man," he said. "Facing the facts and moving through them. Now, dry up. I want to watch at least three episodes before you go pirate on me. *Cah, cah, cah.*"

So we watched the ridiculous show. And I have to admit, I sort of loved it. I even begged my parents to buy me a leather jacket and everything a few months later.

QLT.

Quantum Leap Theory.

You forgot where I was, didn't you? Squashed in the hallway, almost late for what I just discovered was an incredibly amazing class, remember? I had just put up my hands to push back against whoever was about to shove me over the railing when a soft, mildly amused voice said, "Hey, hands down."

"Jocelyn," I breathed.

"What are you doing trying to go downstairs?" she said, glossing over the totally geeky, shameless way I had just said her name. Up close like this, I could see freckles sprinkled across her nose and cheeks. My freckles? They were more like splattered paint than a sprinkle.

"I have to get to class!" I shoved my schedule at her. She squinted at where I pointed. "Look what Gramps signed me up for! I take back anything bad I ever said about the old fart. He's a genius! And now I'm going to be late, since no one will let me go downstairs."

Jocelyn narrowed her eyes. "This is your next class?"

"Yeah," I nodded. "If I could just get there."

"And you're excited about that?"

"Duh! QLT, man!"

"Huh."

"What?"

"It's just not something I would've thought you'd be so thrilled about."

I felt my chin jerk backward a bit. Did she think I wasn't smart enough for Quantum Leap Theory? "Listen, doll. I'm not all good looks and wild sense of humor. I've got a serious side, too."

Her eyebrow cocked when I said "doll." Faintly I heard Alice's voice in my mind, urging me not to call girls that. Maybe I should've listened. But Jocelyn let it go.

"Okay," she said slowly. "But this is the up stairway. You should go to the down stairway to go downstairs." She jerked a thumb at a sign with Up Only written in huge letters hanging to my right.

"This stairway is only for going upstairs?" I said.

Jocelyn nodded. "The down stairs are over there." She pointed down the hall above us.

"But stairs can go both ways," I protested.

"Clearly not. I mean, you're going to be late for your, ahem, awesome elective." She pushed the schedule back to me. The warning bell rang and I looked around, surprised to see the stairway was mostly clear. "Have fun!" she said.

I rushed the rest of the stairs and skidded down the hall to the right room, not bothering to look remotely cool as I tried to piece together the room numbers. No one else was in the hall anymore, anyway.

61

Finally I reached it, threw open the door, and rushed in. "Sorry I'm late!"

There, in front of me, was a huge table covered in fabric, an enormous quilted guinea pig in the middle. (Yes, I went closer to make sure it actually was a quilt with a guinea pig. It was.) Around it were four girls and Miss Singer, each holding a needle and thread. Well, except for Miss Singer, who was so startled by me busting in that her needle was poked into her thumb.

"Oh, dear me," Miss Singer yelped.

QLT was not Quantum Leap Theory.

QLT was Quilting 101.

Gramps was a jerk.

The whole school empties out into the cafeteria at dismissal. Imagine kicking an ant's nest and seeing the little black dots swarm up and out of the nest, running into, over, and past each other. You can almost imagine their shrieks and panic. That's pretty much what happened when the dismissal bell rang, only everyone swarmed into the same space instead of out of it. And replace the shrieks and panic with squeals and cheers. I think I saw someone fall but I didn't see him get back up. I'm pretty sure everyone else just trampled over him. The girl in front of me dropped her shoe, looked over her shoulder at the dozens of people stepping on or over it, and just kept going. I couldn't blame her. When I twisted around to see what happened to the shoe, I slammed into someone in front me. The guy gave me a backward elbow jab and kept going.

I felt a rumble in my back pocket from my phone. I reached behind, accidentally knocking someone's bag, so I could read Alice's text.

How goes day one among the normal folk?

"Watch it!" Whoever I bumped into knocked me back with a hard elbow to the ribs. I ducked into a doorway to text back. Ever since Alice won a writing contest last year, she's become a bit of a grammar queen. I knew she'd call me out on anything less than complete sentences.

Almost killed the bio teach. Most popular kid in school hates me. Sat alone in the bathroom at lunch because I couldn't face the runway of shame that was the cafeteria. Might get the crap kicked out of me on the way to the bus. All in all, a success.

I hit send, then added:

And Gramps signed me up for a quilting class.

Alice's reply was just a smiling poop emoji. She gets me, that girl.

Chapter Six

*B*y *the time* I got on the bus, all I wanted to do was close my eyes and wake up in college. Or at least in my room at Addison, with my Modest Mouse posters and my twin bed and my mouth-breathing roommate, Hector, who never cared how late I kept the light on.

I didn't want to get on a bus and try to figure out which stop was mine. I didn't want to have to figure out which seat I could nab and which was social suicide. I didn't want the bus to pull up to Gramps's '70s bungalow with its first-day-of-school-backpack-wearing yard horse or hear Gramps's stupid cackling about signing me up for quilting. I didn't want to sit on the stiff-as-concrete-and-slightly-less-comfortable couch and think about how this day might've been the worst in my life. And, just a reminder, I went through the whole removing-your-eye surgery. And cancer. And this was still definitely the worst day of my life. Ever.

Pretty much the only thing more annoying than being the one-eyed new guy in middle school is a one-eyed

new guy in middle school throwing himself a pity party. I put my earbuds in and tried to drown out the bus line chaos around me. I knew Jocelyn rode the same bus, so I kept an eye on her rather than try to hear the bus numbers being called. I couldn't seem to stop watching her, so it wasn't all that hard. Except Lash Boy Max caught me staring and glared at me. I twirled my fingers at him in a wave, which had the strange effect of making his face turn purple, but he didn't look at me again.

I turned up the song playing on my phone. One thing I missed already about Addison was the music. Now don't go all weird on me, thinking that because it was a school for the blind all the students were super good at music.

Note to anyone who meets a visually impaired person: Do not—I repeat—do not say something as well-meaning but stupid as, "I bet you've got great hearing, though." This is majorly annoying. Yet it happens so often that there was a huge jar in my dorm that got a dollar added to it every time a student heard this from a clueless stranger. At the end of the year, we raffled off the jar. We called it our Music Lesson Fund.

Here's the deal: God doesn't give visually impaired kids an extra dose of musical inclination as a perk for the crap eyes. It doesn't work that way. But, that being said, music is one of those evener playing fields. And maybe it was just my school—I mean, Addison—in particular, but there was an awesome music department. Even more so, everyone was into making original music or finding cool bands no one else had heard of and then doing covers of their songs.

Not me, though. I can't play an instrument or even, if I'm being honest, clap to any beat all that well. But I could totally one-up anyone on musical discovery. I'm the guy to go to for finding the best tracks for studying. The best for working out. The best for watching a gorgeous girl ignore you from the other side of the jam-packed middle school gymnasium. In fact, I met with the folks at Apple about that whole Genius feature they have on iTunes, the one that suggests songs you might like.

Yeah, I totally made that last bit up. But the rest is bona fide truth. I especially love the bands that no one else really knows about yet or the ones so old that everyone's forgotten them. And here's another little nugget of honesty: I especially like acoustic sad music. You know, the kind that's so bleak and depressing and gut wrenching that you feel like, man, my life is in order by comparison. Like, sure it stinks (literally) to be stuck in this gymnasium with a couple hundred hygiene-challenged kids. And, yeah, my gramps was a tremendous pain in the rump who went out of his way to make my first day miserable. And all my friends were in another state, hanging out together while I took on the role of class freak in a new school. And I was crushing hard-core on a girl who already had a boyfriend. A boyfriend who clearly would've liked me to choke on my own fake eye, I might add. But, hey! It wasn't as bad as this girl singing in my ear about wishing she could turn into a bird and fly away but she's too depressed to get out of her bathtub so she might just drown instead. So there's that.

Anyway, I guess I got a little too into listening to that song and sort of lost Jocelyn for a second. I yanked off the earbuds and, sure enough, my bus number was being called. By the time the teacher standing out on the platform could direct me to my bus ("The numbers are right on the side, kid, just *look*"—pause while teacher notices something is off with my vision, then resumes in much more polite tone—"Oh, I mean . . . it's right there."), the doors were already shut and the driver had shifted from park to drive. I banged on the side of the bus and he opened the doors. "Find a seat," the massive driver practically belched.

Now with a background in boarding school, I'm not all that up to date on the whole where-is-the-cool-place-to-sit-on-the-bus know-how. But I had a hunch it wasn't that empty seat directly behind Bubba the Burpy Driver. So I made my way down the aisle. Near the middle, two seats only had one person in them but the guys in each moved their backpacks onto the empty space in a really obvious no-vacancy sort of way.

Jocelyn was in the very back of the bus, sitting near the window, but was so wrapped up in a whispered, forehead-to-forehead conversation with Max that she didn't appear to see me. But considering how carefully she and Max didn't turn at all toward me, I sort of suspected they saw me but failed to note it. I stood stupidly there for a second at the last row. On the other side of Jocelyn and Max were two guys, heads bent over their phones and earbuds in their ears. They also ignored me with intensity. I don't know what I expected—that Max would suddenly hop up and offer me his seat or that he'd scoot over to make room for me or something—or why I just stood there.

"Get in a *seat!*" the driver croaked.

I made my way back up the aisle, noting the backpacks that once again took residency in what would've been an open seat, and finally sank down just behind Bubba the Burpy Driver.

All in all, I'd say Day One was a rousing success.

Jocelyn and I got off the bus at the same stop, about a half block from our houses.

I didn't get up right away to exit the bus, listening to her argue with Max when he got into the aisle behind her. "Why are you getting off here? Your stop is two blocks away."

"Thought I'd walk it," Max said.

"I've got a lot of homework," Jocelyn said. Max sat back down and I silently cheered.

She didn't say a word to me, just walked by me in a superfast stride. I called her name and she didn't turn at all. It was like she was trying to block me out entirely. At least, she acted that way until the bus pulled down the street and turned the corner. Then, suddenly, her steps slowed a little. I picked up the pace and soon we were beside each other.

"Did you make it to your super awesome quilting class?" she asked, still not looking at me.

"I thought it was quantum leap theory."

"Oh." She smiled. "Like the bad TV series?"

"Yeah," I said.

I had to cross the street to get to Gramps's house. It was such a beautiful, bright early fall day. The trees around us swayed with leaves firmly attached and green. The sky was a perfect blue. The air smelled fresh like the clothes Mom would wash and leave to warm in the sun when we were camping. Or maybe that was just Jocelyn, who now stood close enough that our arms—mine bare in a T-shirt, hers still covered down to her fingertips by her long button-down—brushed as we walked in ever slower strides. Her black hair shimmered in the sunlight. It was the lone perfect moment of this day but for some reason, I felt drained. I don't even know what I wanted. I just knew it wasn't to walk into Gramps's dark house.

"See you tomorrow," I said, looking away from Jocelyn and toward the house. I was sure he'd be waiting by the big window in the living room, laughing like a crow and dying to hear all about my first day as Richie Ryder the Quilter. I took another deep breath before turning from Jocelyn. My feet weighed more than a bucket of bricks as I stepped away from her.

"Wait!" Jocelyn's hand wrapped around my wrist.

I didn't say anything.

"Must've been a rough day. You're not even trying to joke around."

I shrugged.

"I like that. When you're not 'on' so much."

I half-turned back toward her. "What do you mean?"

This time, Jocelyn was the one to shrug. "I like that you're just being you. Not trying so hard to be funny." She let my hand fall.

I turned more so I could see her face. Jocelyn's nose was crinkled up as she stared into the sunlight. She had to be hot in her long flannel shirt, but she tugged on the ends so they covered even more of her hands. I leaned toward her, I don't know why, and was surprised that she didn't jerk away. She sneezed, and it was such a loud, clattering pictures-would've-fallen-off-walls noise that both of us cracked up.

"Are you okay?" I said.

Jocelyn grinned. "Sorry about that."

I again took a half-step closer to her, and again she sneezed. Then hiccupped, making us both laugh. I noticed the General's yellow fur still clinging to my backpack.

"Allergic to cats?" I asked.

Jocelyn nodded. I tossed the backpack a few feet away, and Jocelyn took a deep breath in through her nose.

"That's better!" she said.

It was nice, just standing there with Jocelyn. Then I had to go and ruin it. "You talk to me when it's just the two of us. But anytime Max is around, I'm invisible."

Jocelyn hiccupped again. "Dude, someone with hair that red is never invisible."

I whistled between my teeth. "Listen to you, trash talking."

Jocelyn grinned and sort of skipped backward to her house, still facing me. "Richie?" she called.

"Name's Ryder," I reminded her.

Jocelyn rolled her eyes. This time her hiccup was a little bop of her slender shoulders. "Give Max a break, okay?"

Just like I had thought, Gramps was waiting as I walked in.

"How was your day?" Gramps rushed over to his tweed recliner, acting like he had been there all the time instead of spying on me from the window.

"Fine," I said. I walked through the room to the kitchen and dumped my backpack on the table. Day One for me, but Week Two for everyone else meant no respite from homework. Luckily, we had started to cover algebra at Addison last year. Plus, private school education is much tougher than public, right? So I was sure ten minutes, tops, and I'd be done with the math work. Problem one: *A train traveling thirty miles per hour reaches a town twelve times longer than the length of the train. It takes the train seven minutes to get through the town. How long is the train?*

Man, my parents wasted their money on that private school, didn't they?

"So, you liked all your classes?" Gramps prodded.

"Yep." Maybe I'd do the English homework first. I hadn't been able to read the homework announcement on the white board but the teacher said she'd also have assignments on her website. I used my tablet (thank you, Mom, for the Wi-Fi!) to log onto the site. *Read the first 50 pages of* Angela's Ashes *and compile a list of five initial social issues facing the protagonist.* I pulled the book from my backpack. Maybe Gramps wouldn't seem so bad compared to what Frank McCourt endured.

And then I heard Gramps's *cah, cah, cah* laugh. "Any surprise classes?"

"Nope, all pretty standard." I held the book up to my face to block out his stupid smirk.

Gramps sat down across from me at the table. At the same time, the General jumped to the tabletop, settling, of course, in a ball on my backpack. I tried to pull the bag out from under her, and the fur-devil slammed her claws in my hand. Awesome. Now I'd probably get Cat Scratch Fever and die.

"Got some homework?" Gramps prodded.

I nodded.

"Should I get you some needle and thread? *Cah, cah, cah.*"

"Hilarious, Gramps." Truth be told—and I wouldn't be telling Gramps—quilting wasn't all that bad. Just sitting quietly for an hour, poking fabric with a needle. I even was a bit of a rock star about threading the needle. Everyone else had to squint and close one eye. Me? I could just do it.

"Ah, I wasn't trying to be mean. Just think a boy ought to have a hobby." Gramps stared at me with pale blue eyes. I almost believed him.

"A hobby?" I sighed. "And you thought of quilting?"

Gramps shrugged. The General purred and curled up between his arMs. Now both stared at me. "You're a strange kid, Ryder. How am I supposed to know what's going to float your boat?"

After a lull, where Gramps just sat petting the General, sending clouds of yellow fur through the air, he said, "Seems like you and the girl next door are getting along well."

I shrugged, putting my earbuds back in. "I've got a lot of work to do, Gramps."

"Be careful there," Gramps said. "That girl, she's been—"

I was spared Gramps's dating advice by my phone ringing. Mom. "Hey," I said.

"Ryder! I had hoped to leave early and be there to hear all about your day, but I'm getting swamped here." In the background, I heard clacking sounds and figured Mom was typing while she talked with me.

"It's okay, Mom. No big deal."

"You've got your gramps with you, right?" she asked.

"Yep, we're good."

Clack, clack, clack.

"Are you going to be here for dinner?" I asked.

Clack, clack, clack.

"Dinner? *Mmhmm.*" This is how Mom gets when she's researching. She doesn't hear anything I say, just repeats the last word. It's pretty irritating. But it also has its advantages. I pushed away from the table and headed to my room, away from Gramps.

"I'm just going to walk to school every day, okay? It's only like two miles and a straight shot. Only cross one road. The bus is full."

"Full? *Mmhmm.* That's fine."

"And I'm going to cook the General for dinner."

"Dinner sounds good."

"All right. Off to kill the cat, then."

"Great, Ryder." *Clack, clack, clack.* "See you tonight."

"Bye, Mom."

"Bye." *Clack, clack.* "And Ryder?"

"Yeah?"

"Maybe order some takeout instead?"

About two hours and forty-seven pages of *Angela's Ashes* later, the doorbell rang. I hopped up to grab the cash for the pizza delivery guy, knocked my head into the enormous brass chandelier that looked like it belonged to NASA, and startled the General, who shot off the table with a shriek, which woke up Gramps, who had been drooling all over himself on the couch.

"What is it? What is it, Marlene? What do you need?" he yelped, shooting to his feet. Marlene was my grams, who died when my dad was a baby.

I rubbed the lump on my head and shook off the General, who had attached herself to my ankle as the doorbell rang again. I ignored Gramps.

"Coming!" I called at the door. Man, the pizza delivery guy must be on a tight schedule, judging by the way he was now rapping against the door.

"I'll get the door. It's my house." Gramps elbowed past me.

I pushed him back. "I'm already on the way!" I was so sick of the old man being in my face all the time! Not to mention I had been pushed around plenty at school already today.

"Richie Ryder, let me by!" Gramps stomped on my foot. For real! That crazy old man!

He threw open the door before I could tell him that the few sprigs of hair he had on his shiny head were standing straight up and the tweed pattern of the couch was now embedded on his cheek. I was a half-step behind him, his demon cat still clinging to my ankle, and holding the other throbbing foot in my hand.

And there in front of us wasn't hot, delicious pizza. It was Max and, judging by the luscious lashes on the older man standing just beside him, his dad.

Chapter Seven

Max's dad threw out his arm over Max the way Mom does to me when she has to brake the car suddenly. "Um, sorry to disturb. Is this the Raymond residence?"

"Yes, but I'm not buying cookies or hot dogs or whatever it is Boy Scouts sell." Gramps crossed his arms.

"Gramps, this is a kid from school. Max."

Gramps nodded, making the sprigs of hair standing straight up flop over to the wrong side. "First day of school, already has buddies coming over."

I fell into a massive coughing fit.

"I'm Josh Waters. This is my boy, Max. May we come in?" Max's dad asked.

The traitor cat twirled in between Max's legs as we sat around the dining room table.

Max slumped in his chair, half turned away from the rest of us. Mr. Waters, a broad man whose muscles

bulged around his crossed arms, sat straight in his chair. Gramps kept making stupid jokes. I hoped for instantaneous Cat Scratch Fever and death.

"The thing is," Mr. Waters said, "I got a disturbing phone call after school today from Miss Singer. It seems Max here was bullying Richie Ryder."

"It's just Ryder," I said under my breath.

Mr. Waters continued as if he hadn't heard me. "Miss Singer said Max was poking fun at Richie Ryder's visual condition."

"Yeah, that's something we have to keep an eye on," Gramps said. Then his mouth twitched. "But just one eye, of course."

Mr. Waters's nostrils flared but he didn't say anything.

"It was a misunderstanding," I said. "Lash—I mean, Max—wasn't referring to my eye when he called me a freak."

"You called him a freak?" Mr. Waters's mouth turned dead-man white, he was pressing his jaw together so tightly. Max squirmed more than one of Mom's bugs under his dad's glare.

"Oh, now, I'm sure Richie Ryder deserved it. Kid signed up for quilting class, for Pete's sake. *Cah, cah, cah.*"

"Thank you, Gramps. Real helpful."

"It wasn't like that," Max said. "He was hanging all over Jocelyn and wouldn't back off."

Mr. Waters's chin popped in the air like he had gotten slugged. "Wait. What?" He turned his death glare on me. "You were giving Jocie a hard time?"

"No!" I threw my hands up. "No, man. I was just talking with her."

"I prefer to be called Mr. Waters or sir." Mr. Waters crossed his arMs. This time the muscles bulged a bit more than necessary, I thought.

"And I prefer to be called Your Royal Highness." Gramps had a sudden sharpness to his voice. "Sounds like this was all a misunderstanding. Richie Ryder would never harass Jocelyn. The two of them are buddies. Saw them talking—laughing even—on the way home this afternoon."

This news had very different effects on the Waters men. Mr. Waters's face relaxed back into its normal position. But Max's flamed.

"That's good," Mr. Waters said. "Not that Jocelyn can't take care of herself." This came out a little bit like a warning. He took a deep breath. "The thing is, we've come to make amends. Max, here, has to be in good academic and social standing with his teachers in order to remain a student at our martial arts studio. He's up for a promotion to second dan black belt. If Miss Singer doesn't endorse him, he doesn't test. And then he's off our sparring team. It's that simple." He turned to Max while I processed the fact that the kid who currently looked like he wanted to chop me into bits for talking with his girlfriend could probably do just that with his bare hands.

"You're a black belt?" I asked stupidly.

Max nodded. "Since I was eleven."

"Huh."

"What?" Max snapped. Mr. Waters narrowed his eyes at me, too. Both seemed waiting for me to make some snide comment about martial arts.

"Nothing," I said. "It's just—I sort of pictured you more as football material. You know . . ." I waved my hand toward him. I mean, the guy was pure muscle.

"I didn't want to be on the team," he said.

"Oh, right." I nodded, remembering. "The Guinea Pigs."

Max's jawbone clenched. The General hopped up onto his lap. The two of them glared at me. "I'm sorry I pointed out that you're a freak. It has nothing to do with your eyes."

"Eye," Gramps broke in.

"Um, thanks," I said. "Cool. See you tomorrow." I stood up and moved toward the door, giving a silent prayer of thanks when the Waterses and Gramps followed suit. The General hissed as she slid to the floor.

"If there's ever anything we can do, please let me know," Mr. Waters said. He handed Gramps a business card. I saw a profile of someone doing a martial arts kick on it.

"So you're an instructor?" Gramps squinted at the card. "At WMA?"

"Waters Martial Arts," Mr. Waters filled in. "I'm the owner. Fourth-degree black belt."

I thought about Jocelyn practicing in the front yard the day we moved in. I had a good guess where she took her karate lessons.

"This school of yours? It got any openings?" Gramps asked.

Mr. Waters's eyes raked down the old man's pudgy frame and floppy hair. "We could certainly find a way to accommodate anyone interested in learning the sport in our beginners' lessons. They're led by newer black belts. Most of them are a bit younger than—"

"Anyone, eh?" Gramps cut in. "Even freaks?"

Both Max and his dad's jaws dropped open.

"Gramps, knock it off," I cried, feeling my cheeks flaring red.

"*Cah, cah, cah.*" Gramps smirked at us. "I think lessons—toughening this kid up, you know—would make amends. Don't you think, Richie Ryder? Might be a good hobby."

"I don't think martial arts is really my thing."

"It used to be," Gramps said. "You were an orange belt, I think, before . . ."

"Green," I cut in.

Mr. Waters cocked an eyebrow at me.

"I took tae kwon do lessons before I got . . ."

Here's the thing: I know it's just a word. Cancer. Just a word. But it's a thick, sticky word that gets gunked up in my throat sometimes. So I just finished with, "When I was littler. Like seven. Master Johnson said I was a natural fighter."

Mr. Waters nodded, his lip jutting out. Max crossed his arms and scowled at me.

"But that was a long time ago," I added.

"Yeah," Gramps, with his impeccable timing, laughed. "From the looks of you and that girl, I'd say you're more of a lover than a fighter now." He poked his wrinkly elbow into my ribs. Ribs that Max clearly wanted to snap. In fact, I heard this crunching sound and thought the force of his glare was doing just that—cracking my ribs— before realizing it was just his teeth grinding together.

"I think we could whip you back into shape," Mr. Waters said.

"Nah. I don't think I've got an inner ninja anymore." I forced a grin. The whole idea of it was insane. Me? To prove it, I went into the crane pose and flapped my "wings" like it was the chicken dance.

"Yes, mastering martial arts requires strength, drive, and dedication." Mr. Waters stared hard at me. Seriously,

I felt myself shrinking, arms mid-flap. I wasn't a crane; I was one of Mom's bugs, getting dissected by his glare. "It tasks athletes to focus. You're right. That doesn't seem to be your *thing*." Mr. Waters turned toward the door. Max's smirk felt like he was squashing bug-me under his heel.

Then Mr. Waters suddenly turned back to me. He cocked his head to the side as he took me in. Quickly, I dropped my arms and stood straight. I glanced at Max, who rolled his eyes and groaned softly. "Luckily," said Mr. Waters, cocking his head to the other side, "martial arts also provides those skills. Classes are every weeknight. Come as often as you can, Richie Ryder. Beginners class starts at five-thirty sharp."

"But, Dad—" Max yanked on his father's sleeve. I heard him whisper Jocelyn's name.

"Oh, I think she can handle it." Mr. Waters was the one to smirk this time. Max shook his head at me once and followed his father out the door.

"*Cah, cah, cah.*" Gramps clapped his hands together.

"What have you gotten me into?" I sighed.

"Ah, calm down, boy. Maybe this will help you with your anger issues."

"Me? What anger issues?"

"Exactly," Gramps said just as the doorbell rang again. This time, it actually was the pizza guy.

Chapter Eight

"Give karate a shot. What's the big deal?"

Alice and I had resorted to the lamest of communication options: talking on the phone. Of course, we were FaceTiming, but it still felt foreign to be talking instead of texting with her after not seeing her in months.

"Have you seen *The Karate Kid*?" I asked her. "The original movie, where the kid gets his butt handed to him when he checks out his nemesis's karate studio?"

"Duh. Everyone's parents make them watch that movie," Alice replied. She was sitting in this strange chair shaped like a hand. I think she was in a library or something.

"Yeah," I said, moving through the house toward the living room. "But now imagine I'm the kid about to get his butt kicked, and instead of a fierce old Japanese man at my side, I've got Gramps." I swung out the phone so it captured Gramps in all his leisure-suit-wearing glory as he chomped down a slice of pizza. "See?" I asked.

"Hi, Gramps." Alice waved.

"Hi, Girl in the Phone!" Gramps said around a cheesy bite.

I moved back to my bedroom and shut the door. "See what I mean?"

"He's sweet," Alice said. I should've realized Alice wouldn't see reason with Gramps. After all, she counts a man in a nursing home among her friends. Speaking of which, some girl kept bopping into the screen on Alice's end. "Say hi to Kerica!" Alice moved her iPad so I caught a glimpse of the girl. "Kerica, this is Ryder."

The girl looked up from a sketchbook and nodded but didn't smile. Neither did I.

"Aren't you at Addison?" I asked.

"School ended an hour ago," Alice said. All three of us were quiet for a second. "I've been so excited for you and Kerica to meet. My two best friends!"

Another lull. Look, I know it's dumb and everything, but I didn't like the idea that I was half a best friend. Alice was my closest friend. Period. And I got the feeling Kerica felt the same, based on the not-so-super warm greeting.

Alice's white cheeks pinked a little. "Anyway," she said slowly, "back to karate. I think you should do it. My cousin Sam has a couple friends who do karate. They go to tournaments and everything."

"Sam, the gymnast?" Kerica said in the background. "Aren't he and his friends always getting picked on?"

Great, now OBF (Other Best Friend) was showcasing superior Alice background knowledge. Round One: Kerica.

"Not anymore," Alice said. "I mean, they're sort of picked on. But not for the karate. Sam said it made his one friend super fierce. Like no one would mess with her now."

"Fierce is good. I could use some fierce." I made a fierce face.

"Is he constipated?" Kerica asked.

"You know I can hear you, right?" I said, but maybe not in such a nice voice.

Alice moved the phone so Kerica was just barely in the background. "Sorry, Ryder. Listen, what do you have to lose? I mean, this girl you like, you know she goes to the karate studio, right? So you'll get to know her better. And Lash Boy; it might not hurt to get to know him better, too. Maybe he's not as bad as he seems."

"You make sense, Porcelain," I said slowly, thinking about Jocelyn. "Don't know what I'd do with you."

"Ah, I'd be just as lost without you, Ryder."

Kerica glared at me in the background. Round Two: Ryder.

I ignored Kerica and focused on Alice, instead. "Um . . . hmm. Right. Well, I'll talk to you later, okay?"

"Ryder?" Alice's voice was soft. She moved closer to the screen like she was trying to see me better. Or maybe to block out Kerica. I don't know. "What else is up?"

"Nothing. See you later."

"Come on," she said quietly. "What else is bothering you?"

"Nothing." My voice was stiff. Alice stared at me, her eyes flicking back and forth super fast, the way they do when she's nervous. "It's just Gramps. He said something really stupid."

"What?"

"He said karate would help me with my anger issues." I laughed, but it sounded strange. More like one of Gramps's crow calls. "Like *I* have anger issues."

Alice swallowed and moved back from the screen. "Oh."

"What?" I groaned.

Super low and after too long of a pause, she said, "It's just that—maybe—your anger issue is that you *aren't* angry. I mean, you sort of have a right to be a little angry. But all you do is make everything a joke."

"What would I have to be angry about? Artie?" I grinned, feeling like myself again as I pointed to my fake eye. What was wrong with Alice and Gramps, thinking that not being angry was an actual, for-real problem? "So I don't spend any time looking at the past. So what? I keep one eye forward, all the time."

Alice sighed but smiled. Kerica, on the other hand, burst out laughing in the background.

Round Three: Ryder.

In biology the next day, Miss Singer told us to partner up and review cellular structure facts. Jocelyn turned toward me right away. I played it cool, sliding my desk over near hers and opening up my notebook like it was no big deal. But inside? I was jumping around like the General when Gramps gets the laser pointer out.

"Okay," Jocelyn said. "Eukaryotic cells have proteins with microfilaments and microtubules."

"Right." I scanned the textbook for more details. "And the cytoskeleton provides the framework for the cell." I glanced at Jocelyn, who was supposed to be writing notes. Instead, she was watching me. Okay, she was watching my eyes.

I could imagine what it looked like when I was reading. One eye not moving in sync with the other while scanning the words. I cocked an eyebrow. "Any questions?" I asked.

She shook her head and tugged at the sleeves of her shirt.

"Part of the cytoskeleton is made up of actin filaments. They're like strands that push against each other and are what let the organelles move. When you see actin, think action. Actin, action. Got it?" Again, I caught Jocelyn staring.

She hurriedly picked up her pencil and started scribbling notes. I put down the textbook. "What do you call a fish without any eyes?"

Jocelyn's pencil stopped mid-word. "What?" she said, not looking at me.

"*Fffssshh.*"

Her smile was more of a grimace. "I'm sorry," she said. "I didn't mean to be staring like that."

"No biggie," I shrugged and picked up the textbook again.

She finished writing *action* in her notes. "It's just . . ."

"I get it. You're curious." I picked up my own pencil and sketched the parts of a white blood cell in my notebook. "I'll tell you what happened. I was seven. At a restaurant. Mom said I was too old for chocolate milk but I insisted. The waiter barely stirred in the chocolate sauce, so I got Mom's iced teaspoon and stirred it myself. But I forgot to take it out before taking a drink. Bam! Spoon in the eye."

"Shut. Up." Jocelyn's face paled. "My mom was always warning me about that!"

"Dude, I totally made that up." Then I went and snorted. So suave.

Jocelyn whapped at me with her pencil.

"All right, all right!" I held up my hands. "I'll tell you the truth." I took a deep breath. "It was Christmas of my ninth year and all I wanted was an official Red Ryder, carbine action, two-hundred-shot range model air rifle."

Jocelyn leaned back in her seat and crossed her arMs. "Let me guess: you shot your eye out. I've seen *A Christmas Story*. My uncle plans the family party around when the movie marathon is on TV every year." She picked up her pencil and half turned from me. "If you don't want to tell me, that's fine. It's none of my business, anyway."

Her face got droopy and stiff all at once. Without really thinking it through, I covered her hand with mine to stop the scratch of her pencil. Most of her hand was covered by her long shirtsleeve but where her skin touched mine was soft and warm.

"It was cancer. I was seven."

She was quiet for a second. Around us, kids called out facts to each other. Seats shifted and squeaked on the linoleum floor. The long fluorescent lights above us buzzed. Miss Singer wrote in the notebook she always had with her at the desk in front of us. But somehow all I heard was the thump of my heart. All I felt was the

93

small inch of space where our hands still touched and the soft breeze of her breath as it fell across my arm. The darkness to my right didn't matter at all, because Jocelyn was at my left.

"Will the cancer come back?" She didn't breathe after asking. I didn't think she would until I answered.

"I don't think so. I get scans every year, though." But with planning the move from Addison, we skipped this year's scan. I shook my head, trying to get rid of the thought. Again acting without thinking it through, I added, "I try not to think about it."

"It scares you." It wasn't a question.

I nodded.

"You can't stop thinking about it."

This time *I* didn't breathe. I nodded again.

"I was in . . . an accident. When I was nine."

I didn't know what to say, so I didn't say anything. Wrong move, because a half-second later, Jocelyn moved, yanking her sleeves over her hands and closing her note-book. It took me a bit longer to realize that I hadn't been the one to break whatever spell fell over us. The bell had rang.

"Class is over," Miss Singer said when I still sat there at the desk even as the class emptied.

Two miles doesn't sound like a whole lot when you're convincing your mom that you can walk home from school by yourself instead of taking the bus. But did you know that there are two thousand steps in every mile? So walking home means taking four thousand steps. And if each step is about a second-long, you've got four thousand seconds to think about the beautiful girl who lives next door to you and what might've happened to her when she was nine.

I thought about what I knew—what she had said and what she hadn't said. I thought about the way she pulled her sleeves over her hands and wondered if she had scars on her arMs. What kind of accident would leave scars? I thought of what she said when she told me about Gramps bringing her candy on Halloween, about how nice it was to laugh because everyone is so serious with her. What kind of accident would cause everyone to treat you differently? I thought about Max— how weirdly protective he was of Jocelyn, like it was his job or something. Even Mr. Waters was kind of like that.

At the end of four thousand steps I didn't know anything more than when I had started the trek home— except that I was capable of thinking about nothing but Jocelyn for two miles straight.

Then, there she was, standing in Gramps's driveway, with the same tucking-back-a-laugh smile and dark hair shining in the late afternoon light. Jocelyn's eyes were bright, and for a moment, I felt my heart float right up to my throat at the thought that I had put that brightness in her brown eyes.

"Why weren't you on the bus?" she asked.

"Walking is highly aerobic. Good for the heart. You should try it."

"Maybe I will." She smiled and stepped aside. "Looks like Gramps was busy while we were at school."

And there was the yard horse, backpack gone, replaced with a karate uniform and eye patch.

"The old man's hilarious," I said.

Jocelyn grinned, her face so shining and bright that I wanted to give her something. I wanted to be the one making her smile like that, not the old geezer and his horrible yard horse. Something yellow caught my attention, drooping in the decrepit flower garden around the horse. A huge, sunshiny dandelion, its bloom nearly as wide as my fist. I bent, plucked it, and offered it to Jocelyn.

Her nose crinkled and she folded her arms across her chest. That bright smile faded. "No, thanks."

"It's a flower," I said. "For you."

"It's a weed."

"Don't listen to her," I whispered to the dandelion.

Jocelyn knocked the dandelion out of my hand with a quick swipe of her hand.

"Wow," I said, "not even to class yet and you're show-casing your wax-on, wax-off skills." She made a face at me. "Now you're showing off your ability to roll both eyes. Gotta put the new guy in his place, I guess."

She groaned and turned toward her house, stepping right on the bright yellow blossom. "Get ready," Jocelyn called over her shoulder. "I hear the instructor is tough on newbies."

Chapter Nine

*D*ad *must've been* at his laptop when I sent him an email, because I had a reply almost right away.

From: BuffaloRaymond@depresearcher.com
To: EyeEyePirate@zinger.com
Subject: Re: Life with Gramps

Hey Ryder, sorry to hear my dad's been up to his old tricks. Be thankful you didn't grow up with him. I remember my first sleepover, how he had helped me pack everything up. That night there I was feeling cool at my buddy's house and I grabbed my sleeping bag, tossed it out to unroll it, and out falls a roll of toilet paper and a baby binkie. Everyone made fun of me all night. When I woke up in the morning, the binkie was in my mouth. One of the guys popped it in there while I slept. I didn't talk to my dad for a week.

Man, I haven't thought about that in years. Dad said he thought it'd make everyone laugh, kick off the fun at the sleepover. The man can be clueless.

If he gives you more trouble like that quilting class, just tell your mom. She'll keep him in line. But try not to let him get to you. Old man means well. He's just misguided.

About that girl next door, yeah, I think I do remember hearing something about an accident. She and her brother, I think. Some sort of fire, and he didn't make it out. Sad story. I think they were nine and ten at the time.

Dad was really broken up about it.

All right, gotta get back to the grind. I'm collecting dung samples today. Wish you were here.

—Dad

P.S. About the karate class—what have you got to lose? You were pretty awesome at it before. Never backed down.

Gramps's Goldsmobile shut off with a growl and puff of gray smoke outside Waters Martial Arts studio. I cranked on the handle to roll up the window and spare the ears of the kids walking in from the atrocity of "Disco Duck." (It's a song. For real. YouTube it. On second thought, don't. Just know that it's as terrible as the title suggests. Then picture an old man shimmying his butt in the seat next to you as he quacks along.)

"Ready to knock 'em dead, Richie?" Gramps asked as I opened the door.

I ignored him. "Class is an hour, so you can head home."

I tried to ignore the way his face puckered a little bit and his hand slid from his own door handle. "Oh. All right. See you tonight."

"Bye, Gramps." I felt a smidge guilty and wasn't sure why. I mean, the guy is a jerk to me all the time. Dad's voice rang in my ears, about Gramps being lonely. Maybe the tae kwon horse wasn't a jab but rather a show of support. Maybe he's not awful. Maybe I'm the awful one. I paused and turned around. "Do you, um, want to watch or something?"

Gramps yanked the keys out of the ignition so fast I thought he'd whip himself in the face with them. "Let's go!"

I don't remember much about my last karate studio. I mean, I was only seven after all. (Truthfully, most of my

101

two-eyed memories are blurry. The irony isn't lost on me there.) But I vaguely remember a matted floor. White walls. A lot of trophies in cases. Pretty quiet, except for a couple moms chatting while we went through forms and kicks.

Waters Martial Arts? It was nothing like that. At all.

Music boomed from huge speakers in the back of the room. A hip-hop song melted into punk rock, followed by a guitar-heavy '80s anthem, and then alt-rock. Only one thing was common with each song—intense and fast beats.

"Ah, you're here, Mr. Raymond." Max's dad crossed the huge open gym in long strides. He wore a black belt with a red stripe through the middle. I noticed that as he passed us the kids in his path moved out of the way. One of them called him "Master." I wondered if I'd have to do that. I think "mister" is plenty polite, don't you?

"I told your grandfather on the phone earlier that Wednesdays might be a better day to start, since today is our most intense workout day. Most newbies wait at least a month before taking on Full Throttle Tuesdays." We both turned toward Gramps, who was cackling into his fist. That almost-sorry, nearly-ready-to-bond feeling I had earlier? Whoosh. Gone.

"Maybe you'd like to just watch today," Mr. Waters suggested. Just then Max passed by to get a drink from the water fountain. But first he snickered.

My chin popped up. How hard could it be? I don't mean to brag, but I can run a mile in under seven minutes. Top of my class at Addison.

"No, I'd like to start today," I said.

This, I soon realized, was both the right and wrong thing to say.

It was right, because Mr. Waters's eyebrow arched again. His bottom lip jutted out a bit and he nodded. For the first time ever, it felt like I wasn't a boogie stuck in his nose but an actual person. "I admire that, son," he said.

Max choked on his gulp of water.

But it was also the wrong thing to say because Full Throttle Tuesdays were designed by the devil. We had to run through different stations in groups of five, staying at each for five minutes at a time. These stations included standing up only to fall back down into push-ups, then popping back up to do it all over again, kicking targets, standing in a squat and punching the air in front of us, and alternating between panicking that your lungs would explode and wishing for said explosion. By the time I got to the plank station, I was grateful to stick to one position.

The whipped cream to top this suck sundae was that all of this was led by Peggy, a black belt in pigtails who might've been ten years old. "Dig!" Peggy bellowed at us as she skipped—skipped!—between stations. "Dig!"

You might think I'd whine a little. Maybe even cry or collapse or, worse yet, quit. No way, man. And this was crazy—totally insane—because I hurt all over. But not once did I slow or grimace or pause. And not because I'm in super shape or anything. Not even because I had something to prove to Master Waters or Gramps or Max.

I'm having trouble describing it but somewhere in the push-ups and the puddles of sweat, I lost myself and just became this body. This body that went through motions and pushed and even pulsed with the music that pumped through the air. This body that was listening and doing what I wanted it to do, not making me a product of what it inflicted on me.

Not that I wasn't tired. I mean, my glasses fogged up. My muscles melted to goo. My arms flopped instead of jabbed by the end of five minutes. I'm pretty sure the moves I was doing weren't the real moves, either. I wasn't entirely sure I wasn't going to throw up the chicken noodle soup I had eaten before class. But somehow I pushed that all aside and I was just *there*, following Peggy the Pint-Sized Punisher's squeaky demands to "Dig! Dig! Dig!"

Maybe I could go all philosophical about it. Later that night, lying in bed, I sort of did, I guess. I mean, for a while after getting Artie, Mom and Dad made me go to this therapist. I had to sit in an office in front of this roundish man with deep dark circles under his eyes, accentuated by even darker thick glasses, and talk. I felt as if I were at the zoo, visiting the panda exhibit, except the animal kept asking, "How do you *feel*?" in a low, drawn-out voice. Anyway, nothing the therapist said really stuck with me except for this: "You're allowed to feel however you feel. Let yourself feel it." He had shifted in his chair and added, "And however you feel is *normal*."

I remember that because, frankly, it's total crap. Total. Crap.

You don't have to feel bad if you don't want to. I repeat: you don't. You don't have to feel sad or angry or mad. You don't. I mean it. You just decide, "Nope." That's what I did. I decided that while looking at the sad panda man. I wasn't going to wallow or be angry or whatever else would be a "normal" feeling. I was going to laugh. Mom brought the therapist a bamboo plant during our last session, so glad and relieved that I was so happy after just a few sessions. Therapy Panda warned that I'd need to deal with my emotions eventually, but you know what? That was seven years ago. Half my life ago! And I'm still doing just fine.

But do you remember where I was now? In the middle of Full Throttle Tuesday, doing knee drops across the mat, trying not to slip in my own puddle of sweat.

Sorry if I distracted you with that digression, but for some reason, Therapy Panda popped in my head. And I think it was because, right then, I wasn't trying to feel—or *not* feel—anything. I was just moving. No worries about doctor appointments. No jealousy over old friends making new friends. No crushes on beautiful, unavailable girls next door. No anger at stupid old men and stupider yard horses with eye patches. No nothing.

And it was awesome.

Toward the end of class, as I limped to the water fountain, Master Waters fist bumped me. Max, standing just behind him, carefully ignored me.

"Great job out there, son," Master Waters said. "I haven't seen so much potential in a kid on day one in a long time. Can't wait to see you in the sparring ring."

Later, I was pretty freaking thrilled at the compliment. But in the moment, I was just trying to stand upright.

"You and me both," Max muttered. He popped a plastic mouth guard between his lips and trotted out to the advanced sparring class starting behind us. All of the students wore foam padded helmets and padding on their hands and feet. Some of the fighters wore harder chest protection, too. In pairs, they kicked, punched, and pummeled each other. I sank into the seat next to Gramps to watch—and, okay, to gain the strength to stand again.

This one kid was smaller than the rest but with moves that were like a blur. The opposing fighter ducked and blocked as best he could but was no match for the smaller fighter who just took the hits and barreled ahead with pure aggression. The fighter's leg pumped kicks without ever dipping to the ground. *Whap, whap, whap* into the bigger kid's side and then a slice through the air to land a hit to the head.

"Wowza," Gramps muttered beside me.

The bell rang, ending the match, but the fight kept going anyway, the smaller fighter rushing the larger fighter, who finally must've had enough. As the smaller fighter rushed him, he lifted his leg in a quick side kick, sending the smaller fighter flying backward to land sprawled on the mat.

I was so caught up in the fight, I hadn't noticed Master Waters's scary purple face. Without even checking to see if the kid was okay, he yanked the smaller fighter upright and screamed, "What the hell were you thinking? Never rush into a kick! How many times do I have to tell you? You've got to fight with your head, too!"

I sucked in my breath as the kid reached up to pull off the helmet. The sleeves of the kid's uniform slipped down, the fluorescent lights making the puckered white scars shine.

And I knew who it was before the helmet was off. Jocelyn. She sucked in air, her shoulders rising with the effort. Funny, I had always thought she seemed thin and sort of delicate. But now I knew. She was strong and tough as braided wire.

And apparently in major trouble with Master Waters, who looked ready to throttle her again. "What's wrong with you today?"

"I don't know," Jocelyn said. She shook her head, letting her black hair swing around her head. "I'm sorry. I'll concentrate more next time." She slipped a hand up under the chest gear, rubbing at her ribs, where the larger fighter had kicked her. Max took a half step toward her, his eyes narrowed on that spot.

The larger fighter—I recognized him now from the halls at school—held out a hand to shake Jocelyn's. "Sorry if I hurt you," he said, eyes flicking to Max and back to Jocelyn. I think he was apologizing more to him than her.

"No, no," she said. "My fault for rushing you. Stupid rookie mistake."

Master Waters crossed his arms and nodded. "Good word choice. You're on rookie duty." He turned his back on Jocelyn.

"Wait!" Jocelyn called out at the same time Max said, "What?"

Master Waters didn't bother turning back to them, just tapped two other fighters on the shoulders and reset the timer. "I mean it, Jocelyn. You're in charge of training the newbies. Until you can focus on control, you're not sparring. In fact," he said, glancing over at me, where I suddenly felt like a boogie all over again, "you can start training again when someone in the beginners' class reaches the point where he or she can spar."

"But that takes weeks!" Jocelyn snapped. Max shook his head at me like this was all my fault. Again, I did something both very smart and very stupid. I grinned at him and winked. Smart, because it felt amazing, especially when his head practically imploded, going all sorts of scary colors before settling on white. Stupid, because I was pretty sure he'd murder me at his first opportunity.

"You have a death wish, Richie Ryder?" Gramps muttered. "That boy looks like he wants to break your face into splinters. I just saw him break a board. He could do it, boy. He could turn your face into splinters."

I sighed. "I'm just messing with him. He thinks I'm after his girlfriend."

Gramps nodded and crossed his hairy arMs. "Which you are."

I shrugged and Gramps laughed like a crow. "When he breaks your face into splinters, I'll pick up a piece or two—maybe one with a freckle—to send to your dad. Give him something to remember you by."

I elbowed the old man, trying to quiet his cackling enough to listen to Master Waters.

"Yeah, it might take weeks. Or longer," he was telling Jocelyn, his back still to her. "Depends on the student and your ability as the teacher. For now, that's you, Jocie."

"Oh, come on!" she whined.

Wrong move. Master Waters turned around suddenly.

She was still doing push-ups when Gramps and I left a couple minutes later.

Chapter Ten

*H*ere's another *bad* joke for you: What's black and white and red all over?

Answer: A half-eaten zebra.

I know, I know. I should be dodging rotten tomatoes for that one. If you've never read a joke book, the real answer is supposed to be newspaper. (Get it? "Red" is actually "read.")

While I don't have a lot of experience with half-eaten zebras (at least not yet. Who knows what Dad will turn to once he's bored with buffalo?), I do know a lot about newspapers. A perk about having two scientist parents is being wicked good at researching. When I wanted to learn more about what caused all those scars on Jocelyn's arms, I headed to the school library, logged onto the local newspaper's website, and searched. I entered "fire," "children," and Jocelyn's last name into the search bar.

The first thing to pop up was a picture of a boy. It was just a square shot of a smiling face, black and white,

111

but I knew right away he was Jocelyn's brother. He had the same dark eyes, same dusting of freckles over his nose. Yet I could tell, just from the smiling picture, that he was different to her, too. He smiled like he was the sun, blazing to the cusp of a burn. Does that make sense? Sorry, we were reading sonnets in English class just before lunch.

I almost shut down the computer right then. I even opened a new tab and started to log onto YouTube, thinking I'd watch someone play Minecraft or something instead. I didn't want to read about how that smiling face belonged to a boy. A boy who had died. But I clicked back to the article that ran with the picture.

A young Papuaville boy died and his sister was severely burned Tuesday in a fire that began where they played in a small shed. Papuaville Fire Company firefighters struggled to contain the flames.

Police say Jacob Andros, 10, perished from smoke inhalation after he and his younger sister, age 9, and a neighborhood friend, also age 9, turned a backyard shed into a play fort. Jacob Andros toppled a kerosene heater kept in the shed. Police were not able to share why the heater was on at the time.

"We suspect the deceased lit the heater himself," Police Chief Frank Williams said.

The spreading flames kept the children from escaping through the shed door. The other boy crawled out a window he appears to have broken open, but police speculate that Jacob Andros and his sister attempted to put out the fire themselves. The escaped child ran inside the home of Margaret Andros, the siblings' mother. She attempted to free the trapped children, while the escaped boy called the fire department.

"I have no doubt that we would have had two lost lives if it weren't for that call to the fire department," Williams said.

I stopped again. I fought the urge to just close the webpage. Did I even have a right to know these details— to learn about the ugliest part of Jocelyn's life? I rubbed at my eyes (okay, fine, eye) with the heel of my hand and thought about Jocelyn flinging herself against the person she was sparring in karate. Of course she stayed and tried to fight the flames. I thought about this unnamed boy who had saved her. I had an idea who that might have been. Wasn't Max still trying to save her, every chance he could?

I turned back to the article.

Margaret Andros suffered minor burns to her arms and torso from pulling her daughter from the burning shed. The daughter sustained severe burns. The mother was only able, however, to retrieve the younger child before the fire consumed the walls of the shed, her son still trapped inside.

"While Margaret Andros undoubtedly acted on instinct to protect her children, she should've waited for the fire department," Williams said. "She put herself at great risk."

Fire fighters were on the scene within minutes but by then the boy had perished, most likely from smoke inhalation, Williams said.

"Let this be a powerful lesson to the communities," Williams said. "This mother believed her children, at ages 9 and 10, knew not to play with matches. But Jacob used a box of matches to light the kerosene heater. Fire safety is a message families should continue reiterating with their children throughout their lives."

Margaret Andros was released from the hospital last evening but her daughter remains in critical care.

I clicked on a smaller image at the bottom of the article page. Up popped a picture of a still-smoldering shed, the kind Gramps had in the backyard to house his lawn-mower. A yellow bicycle with a white basket attached to the front lay on its side just outside the shed. I zoomed in on the basket. Dandelions tumbled out of it in a for-gotten, wilted heap.

I should've closed the article right away instead of star-ing off into space like an idiot with it on my screen, wishing I could go back and never read what happened to Jocelyn and her brother. Wouldn't it be better to never find this out, to never have to think about a little kid going through something like this? Wouldn't it be better to find out when—and only when—Jocelyn shared it herself? Man, I was such a jerk, always having to push things too far. Now that I knew, what next? What was I supposed to do with this information?

I took off my glasses and rubbed at my eye again. It didn't matter, of course. I still saw the article just as well as I had before. My glasses aren't to correct my vision anyway. The tumors made my vision acuity twenty-sixty to twenty-seventy, instead of twenty-twenty, but the glasses didn't fix that at all. They're just clear lenses, but the doctor (and my parents) insist I wear them, to give another layer of protection for my good eye.

But I sort of wished now that taking off my glasses made my vision blur. What if I slipped up and dropped in conversation something like, "Oh, sort of like that time you and your brother were in that fire and he died?" Okay, that's not likely to happen. And now I'm feeling like even more of a jerk for even thinking that.

I am such a jerk.

Such.

A.

Jerk.

I don't think anyone sighed as heavily as I did just then. It sort up bubbled up from my toes, making my ribs hurt as I heaved it out of my nose.

Mega-sigh, and the fact that she came up on me from the right, totally covered up Miss Singer's approach. I jumped about a half-foot in the air when her fingers patted my shoulder. Then I squeaked like a squirrel and she jerked her hand back so fast that she slapped herself in the face with the notebook she carried.

And that's how I gave my bio teacher a bloody nose.

A few minutes later, Miss Singer sat beside me pressing a tissue to her nose.

"I'm really sorry," I said. "I didn't mean—"

"Nah, it's my fault." She sniffed and checked the tissue for blood. When she saw that it had stopped, she nodded to herself. Miss Singer must take this quilting business seriously. Today she was wearing a quilted vest covered in frogs, their legs outstretched. I vaguely hoped she'd wear it later in the year when we did dissections. "I should've said something instead of just approaching you like that. I forgot about the whole . . ." She jabbed a thumb toward her eye.

"Oh, right." I clicked off the article, embarrassed to have been caught reading it.

"That was a terrible time," she said, pointing at the computer screen.

"Was—was he one of your students?" I asked.

Miss Singer nodded. "I stopped teaching kindergarten after his death. Even though it had been years since he was in my class, everywhere I looked in the classroom, I saw Jacob." She pulled the edges of her vest closer and sort of shuddered. "Every time, it felt like ripping off a scar. He's—he *was*—one of those kids you never forget. A kid who will always be one of *your* kids, as a teacher."

I didn't know what to say, so I didn't say anything for a long time. Probably it was only a few seconds, though. "Would you mind not mentioning . . ." I chewed my lip for a second. "It's just, Jocelyn never told me about it herself, and I don't want to . . ."

Miss Singer shuddered again. "I'm not going to bring this up to Jocelyn, Richie Ryder. You don't need to worry about that."

She ran her thumb around the cover of her notebook. It was one of those leathery type ones—moleskin, I think it's called. "I probably shouldn't say anything like this to a student, but speaking with you just now about Jacob? It's the first time I've ever said his name without crying. That's why I have this." She lifted up the notebook. "My therapist, he suggested writing down my feelings."

I rolled my eyes. "Therapists," I said. "I had to go one for a while, after Artie." I pointed to my fake eye when she looked confused. "Useless."

"Not always." Miss Singer lowered the notebook. "I find it helpful, putting my thoughts into print. Makes them organized. Makes them real."

"Whatever works," I said. "And no worries, I won't mention it. You won't either, right?"

"Here's the thing," Miss Singer said softly. "A part of Jocelyn is always going to be stuck in that horrific shed. We don't need to worry about bringing it up, about what it would do it her. She's already there."

A rush of chatter from the library door being opened to masses of students in the hall broke up the quiet between us. Miss Singer glanced at the clock.

"What time is it?" I asked. For a second, Miss Singer's brow wrinkled in a look-for-yourself expression. But, of course, then she remembered I couldn't see the clock on the wall.

She swallowed. "About two minutes before the bell. You should shut this down," she said, gesturing to the computer.

I took her advice, determined to get to history class before the bell for the first time yet. But the computer took forever to shut down and then I had to make a pit stop by my locker for books. I still had a cool minute leeway to get to class, but then I passed Jocelyn in the hall and she gave me a sideways grin and time slowed for a moment, or maybe it was just me. So I ended up not at all ahead of masses of students and instead just smack dab in the middle of them.

"Mr. Raymond," my history teacher, Mr. Sidewick, droned as I came in late. Again. "What's the explanation today?"

Here's the thing: history class was on the second floor, right in the middle of the hall. Let me tell you why this stunk. First, there were identical lockers lining both sides of the classrooms and students darting in and out of them like adrenaline-junky chipmunks rushing across the road. I literally didn't see them until I was stepping on top of them. Second, even though I knew history was the fourth door on the left, the rush of students made it super tough to count the doors. Third, I had the class with Lash Boy, who always seemed to be lurking right inside the door, watching me. (Okay, fine. He was there because his assigned seat was the one right by the door. But still, it felt like he was watching me. Or, more specifically, watching me walk right by the classroom and doubling back.) The alternative was fighting through the crowds to zero in on the room numbers and then moving to the next one. Would it kill Mr. Sidewick to hang a poster or something on the door? But nope, he was as boring as his subject. No way to distinguish his classroom from any other.

"I missed the door," I mumbled.

"Would you like me to take its picture? Text it to you, maybe?" Mr. Sidewick crossed his arms and fought a smile as the rest of the class laughed.

"Take a picture," this dumb-as-rocks kid who sits next to Max sniggered. "Hear that, Max?"

Max didn't say anything.

I called Mom as soon as I got home. Gramps wasn't there and he was always home. Mom wasn't, either. It felt weird, like I was an imposter, to be at Gramps's house without anyone else. Just the General was there, staring at me with vicious, evil eyes from the doorway of whichever room I entered. It would be a long shot to reach Mom. Lately, she'd been coming home later and later as her research took off. Last night, I felt her brush my hair off my forehead with butterfly-feet-light fingertips hours after I had fallen asleep on the couch. (I woke up with a rash. Not from Mom, of course. From the nubby couch that had been gathering dust since 1976.)

I called her anyway, mostly to ask about dinner, but, okay, fine, also because I was creeped out at being in Gramps's house alone with the General.

Only, when the call connected with her phone, I heard it buzzing from her bedroom. She had forgotten it. Great.

I hung up on my end and went into her room to find the phone. I'm not sure why. I mean, I guess it was sort of nosy of me. But I wanted to see how many missed calls she had. Dad hadn't called me in a couple days and I wondered if he was too busy to call her, too. I was throwing myself another little pity party. Whatever.

Mom's room was super neat. Her bed was made with the sheets tucked tightly. The window shades were open to let in as much light as possible. Her phone was the only thing other than a lamp on her nightstand. A soft breeze from the open windows made the flowers on her dresser flutter. Dad sent her flowers every week, and she always kept them in her room. Never in the living room where Gramps and I could see them, too. For some stupid reason, I wished the wind would knock the daisy bouquet right over. I picked up the phone. One other missed call, with voicemail, but it wasn't Dad. It was my oncologist, Dr. Carpenio.

Even though we moved around a lot, we always kept the same ocular oncologist right in the DC area where I had been first diagnosed. At screenings, I had an MRI, had my eye dilated, and was then scrutinized by the doc. Bloodwork, too. It was a long, boring day.

All right, fine. I lied there. It wasn't boring at all. It was scarier than being stalked by a demonic cat to have a doctor actively look for what else could be wrong with you. I hate it. Hate it. Just seeing the caller ID on the phone made my hands get sweaty and my heart flop down into my gut. For a second, I wondered if somehow Dr. Carpenio somehow felt that my remission was over. *That's stupid,* I told myself. *He hasn't seen me in more than a year. How would he know?* But my idiot heart stayed put, drowning in stomach acid.

I wasn't really thinking as I listened to Mom's voicemail. I know it was the wrong thing to do. I mean, it's *her* phone. But still, I listened to the message: *Dr. Raymond, it's been more than a year since Ryder's last exam. We'd like to schedule a visit as soon as possible. Please contact Dr. Carpenio's office and we will schedule our next available appointment for Ryder.* Still not really thinking, I hit the delete button.

I about jumped out of my skin at the voice that came trickling through Mom's open window. "I know, I know."

Only it wasn't a creepy you-just-got-caught "I know." It was a sad you're-right-and-I'm-awful-and-wrong "I know." The type I'd be saying when Mom found out what I had just done. The thing was, it wasn't me being caught right now. I put the phone back where it was and hot-tailed it out of Mom's room to see who Gramps was talking to outside.

When I got to the front door, I saw that he was alone, kneeling down in front of the yard horse to pick weeds in the flowerbed circling the cement horse. He had planted some purple mums around the horse's hooves. And now, apparently, he was talking to said horse.

"He's more like me than he is his dad. You know how Tom would always clam up? Storm off to his room? Richie, he never backs down. Always pushes back. Usually with a joke." Gramps snorted, like the yard horse said something back to him.

Great. He's demented.

"You're right, of course," said Gramps, throwing another dandelion in the pile behind him. "He's covering up what's bothering him with all those bad jokes. 'Course he is. Don't know where he gets that. *Cah, cah, cah.* Yeah, I know. Going to have to face it sooner or later. But enough 'bout that. Since it's nearly October, how about I add a rake to this here horse's arms?"

Gramps whistled softly, which is probably why he didn't hear as I eased open the screen door. I stepped onto the patio. If he wasn't talking to the yard horse, who was he talking to? I got my answer a second later.

"Well, now, Marlene," he said as he positioned a rake across the horse's upright arms, "I can just about hear you laughing at this getup." Then the old man bent to gather up his gardening tools, but instead of picking them up, he sort of crumbled next to them. I almost rushed to him but I heard the suck of air into his lungs and a sob. "I miss you, Marlene. You'd think I'd be done missing you by now, but I miss you more now than ever."

His big, dirt-splattered hands rubbed at his head, knocking his huge gardening hat sideways. "I don't know how to be a grandpa any more than I knew how to be a dad."

I eased the door back open and let it slam shut, pretending I was just now stepping outside.

"Hey, Gramps," I called. "What's up?"

Gramps's back stiffened for a second before he pushed himself back to his feet. "Just keeping up with the landscaping," he said. "Got to keep the place respectable looking."

"Are we looking at the same thing?" I said, even though I immediately wished I hadn't, since the old man's face turned as stony as the yard horse. But I mean, come on. We're talking about a giant cement horse wearing a gardening hat, complete with ears poking out of the top, and holding a rake, surrounded by purple mums.

Man, I can be such a freaking jerk sometimes.

The thing is, I didn't even realize how much of a jerk I was until after we sloshed through another round of takeout—Chinese food, which Gramps ordered by asking me, "Which Oriental rice do you want?" despite me rolling my eye and groaning—and got in the enormo car to go to martial arts.

Even then, the whole ride there, I didn't realize the depths of my jerkiness.

It wasn't until Gramps turned on the ignition and immediately punched the off button on the stereo that I really looked at the old man. I don't mean "old man" in a he's-a-grandpa way. I mean, he suddenly looked *old*. Not cackling to awful jokes, bopping to bad tunes, or smirking in his '70s glory. Just old.

"Um," I said as he pulled into a parking spot, "do you want to come in?"

He shook his head. "Your mother will pick you up after class."

"Oh, okay," I said. "See you later."

But he didn't even say goodbye.

Chapter Eleven

*D*ad called while I was in the middle of practice warm up.

I heard the ringtone—a buffalo braying—and stopped mid-jumping jack to grab the phone. Finally, Dad within calling range!

"Where are you going?" my instructor, aka Jocelyn, barked at me. The dozen other kids froze with arms up and legs spread mid-stretch, mouths open, everyone facing me. Jocelyn crossed her arMs. For a second, I thought I saw smoke billowing out of her flared nostrils.

"Um, it's my dad." I jerked my thumb toward my duffel bag where my phone was stashed.

"I don't care if it's Taylor Swift, you don't leave the mat without permission."

Now on its sixth ring, the phone brayed again. "Okay," I said, and flashed her my sweetest smile. Dimple and everything. "May I have permission to answer the phone?"

Definite smoke from nostrils. "No."

"Are you serious, doll?" Wrong move.

One hundred sit-ups, fifty push-ups, and a five-minute plank later, I began to thoroughly wish I had taken Alice's advice not to call girls "doll" anymore.

The worst part? Everyone in the class had to do the extra work because of me. I swear, I felt the back of my head swelter under their glares. After the extra drills, Jocelyn ran us through forms—an orchestrated set of fight movements.

"You know we're a sparring school," she told the class after we went through the first five moves twenty times in a row. "But no one here gets to spar until you're at least a yellow belt. To become a yellow belt, you need to know the basics."

Let me tell you—I totally nailed the form. I picked it up way quicker than most of the people in the class, not that Jocelyn acknowledged it. Or that I pointed it out or anything. I was too busy trying not to make eye contact with anyone else. After class, an older man—maybe Dad's age—slapped his hand down on my shoulder. *This is it,* I thought. *They're turning on me!*

"Good job, son," he said. "Being a newbie is tough. I actually tried to get a drink of water mid-class. Master Waters made us do drop-knees for fifteen minutes straight."

"Dude, I know who's going to keep the phone on silent mode from now on," another guy in his twenties said.

"Gotta tell you," a girl about my age confessed as she wiped sweat from the back of her neck, "I forgot to turn off my phone and I was sweating more at the idea it would ring than I was from the workout!"

I smiled at them, grateful they weren't clobbering me. "Thanks, guys."

"Can you believe Miss Andros's face when new guy called her doll?" The girl laughed to the others. Took me a bit to realize that Miss Andros was Jocelyn. "OMG."

They trickled out of the studio one by one. Soon it was just me waiting for Mom. I texted her and even broke down and actually called her, only to have no response. Too late. I remembered she had left her phone at home. I was stranded.

I considered calling Gramps, despite the evil eye he had given me earlier, but then Jocelyn came from the back of the studio wearing her sparring gloves. Again and again she punched a target.

"Miss Andros!" I called.

She paused and sighed. "No one else is here, Ryder. You can call me Jocelyn."

I kicked off my sneakers. "Can I hold a target for you while I wait for my mom to pick me up?" I asked.

She shrugged. "All right."

Fifteen minutes later, Mom still wasn't there, and I was an expert-level handheld target holder. I held the target perpendicular to the ground to catch Jocelyn's wicked fast ridge-hand hit (think: hand stretched out taut and whipped into the target). She hit the target so hard my hand went flying. The second I got it back in place, she whipped it again.

"Want to have your butt kicked?" she asked between huffs of air. But she didn't say butt, if you know what I mean.

"Excuse me?" And here's the thing: maybe my voice cracked there. A lot. Maybe I backed up in a hurry, too.

Jocelyn's head jerked back and for a second she was statue still. Then she burst out laughing. Not a cutesy giggle, either. A bellowing, massive can't-breathe guffaw. "Let me try that again," she said. "I said, 'Want to hold an axe kick?' *Axe* kick." She demonstrated, lifting her leg straight up to her shoulder and ramming it down in a straight line. "That's an axe kick. I asked if you'd hold the target for one."

Still softly laughing, she wrapped her fingers around my wrist and turned it so I was now holding the target parallel to the ground. In slow motion, she did the kick onto the target.

"Oh, right," I said, shrugging my shoulders. I tried to play it cool but couldn't. "You know I almost wet myself, right?"

Jocelyn snorted, then erupted into the bellowing again.

"And you sort of sound like a donkey when you laugh," I added.

She held her stomach and bent at the waist. "If you could've seen your face!"

"You're scary, okay? You're really scary." At that moment, though, she was just beautiful. Her shoulders rising and falling with laughter. Her face shining and red, hair plastered to her forehead with sweat. She looked so . . . happy.

Of course, I ruined it. "I heard about what happened to you. To you and your brother."

Jocelyn again turned to a statue. Her face, so shining and happy just a second before, now looked distorted. Like her face didn't know how to shift so quickly from joy to sorrow.

"I'm sorry," I said lamely. "I wish I didn't . . ." I took a deep breath. "I'm sorry," I said again. "It really sucks . . ."

For the longest second ever, Jocelyn kept that statue pose. Then she nodded. "Yeah, it does." Gently, not really into it, she lobbed another axe kick onto the target I held. Soon she was back to her usual pace of whamming the target. I stood there, my stupid tongue thick and useless, wishing I could think of something to say instead of just blurting the worst possible thing. *It really sucks.* Who freaking says that? Me. I wished Mom would show up.

131

Eventually Jocelyn stopped, out of breath again. I thought this would be it, where she told me she hated me and asked me not to come back to Waters Martial Arts.

Instead, she ran her hands through her hair, flicking the sweat off her fingers. She smiled softly and looked at me straight on. Not doing that odd flickering look most people do when they know about Artie. Just a straight-on look. "Most people," she said, "when they find out, they say something like, 'Everything happens for a reason,' or something equally stupid. But they should say what you did, you know? That it sucks. Because it does. It sucks."

She grabbed the target from my hand and held it outright. "All right, so you saw about a thousand ridge hand hits. Let me see one."

I didn't say anything back, just stared at her stupidly for a second or two. Then I slammed into the target. Next to the powerful thuds she had generated, my ridge hand was pathetic. Her arm didn't even move. But she didn't laugh at me or comment on how much redder I'm sure my face just got. Jocelyn talked me through pivoting my hips and shifting my weight into my shoulder instead of my hand. Neither of us stopped, even as the door to the studio opened and closed and the advanced class trickled in. Around us, they began their own warm-ups.

Speaking of warming up, my glasses got so foggy, I tossed them on top of my duffel bag.

"Can you see without them?" Jocelyn paused.

I nodded, feeling my hair damply flop on my forehead. "Yeah, they're just plain lenses, no prescription or anything."

Jocelyn's forehead crinkled, so I explained. "Sort of a protect-the-spare idea. Since I only have one eye, I wear glasses all the time to give Artie a little boost in protection. If something happens to my good eye, I'd really be screwed."

Jocelyn's mouth popped open for a second, then closed. "That stinks," she said quietly.

This time I shrugged. "No biggie." And it's not. Wearing glasses I don't need is the least of what sucks about my situation. I didn't mention my left eye already has a lowered acuity thanks to the tumors docs zapped when I was kid, but glasses can't fix that. Or that I get headaches when I have to read too much or stare too long at the computer. Or that I didn't know if the headaches were visual fatigue or the end of my remission. Or that I deleted Dr. Carpenio's message.

I hit the target a little harder after that.

"Can I ask you a question?" Jocelyn asked as I gulped down some water a few minutes later.

133

I braced myself for the do-you-have-superhuman-hearing question. Instead, her eyebrow popped up. "Why do you call it Artie?" She pointed to my fake eye.

Half my mouth pulled back in an involuntary smile. "Artie, like *art*ificial *eye*." I flicked water from my bottle toward her, making her laugh.

"Does it have to have a name?"

"Don't listen to her, Artie," I whispered, cupping my hand toward Artie. "Of course you deserve a name." Dropping the whisper, I said, "I worked through a ton of names, but they just didn't roll off the tongue the way Artie does."

"Oh, really?" Jocelyn crossed her arms like she thought I was teasing her.

"No, I'm serious!"

"Like what?"

"Um, well, first it was sham sphere. Then synthetisphere. Concocted cornea." I leaned against the benches and crossed my arMs. "None of those are real names, you know? Too much of a mouthful."

Jocelyn nodded. I saw her lips twitch like she wasn't sure it'd be okay to laugh. "Did you consider Eye-rene? Or Eye-velyn?"

I tilted my head at her. "Are you implying that my eye is a girl?"

"If the shoe fits," Jocelyn hiccuped. "Or socket, I guess."

"You're a terrible person, you know that?" I shook my head in mock judgment as Jocelyn cracked up.

Huh. Wouldn't have pegged her as a snorter.

By the time Mom finally showed up, rushing through the door with hands fluttering—"I'm so sorry! I'm so sorry! Lost track of time!"—I had mastered the axe kick, too. Jocelyn had me doing drills of ridge hands into axe kicks. I felt, more than saw, Max watching us. Master Waters, however, was right next to us, arms crossed and obviously watching.

"Good job," he said after I asked Jocelyn if it was okay to leave. I wasn't sure who he was complimenting—me for working so hard or Jocelyn for the training.

"Wow," said Mom, when I jogged off the mat, stopping just in time to turn and bow toward Master Waters like I had seen other kids do before leaving. Mom handed me my glasses, lenses wiped clean. Behind us, kids shouted and grunted as they fought.

"Some of those punches looked fierce. Remind me to order you some goggles," she said.

Yeah, like that's going to happen. No way would I be reminding her to buy something that would make me and Artie stand out even more than we already did.

Gramps was in his recliner, the General curled on his lap, when we got home.

A sinking feeling in my stomach churned away when I saw him. Yeah, the old man's a pain in the axe kick, but he's not all bad, right? I sat down on the couch closest to his chair.

"Hey!" I said, shimmying my butt a little. "I sank a little! We're breaking in the couch!"

Gramps swiveled away from me.

Fine. I guess he still wasn't talking to me.

I texted Dad.

Sorry I missed your call.

After about ten minutes, I tried again.

Dad, can u talk?

Nothing. I put my phone on the super lacquered coffee table and tried to tune into Gramps's "program" (that's old man speak for show). This one was a quiz show where families tried to be first to answer questions correctly. They all high-fived each other or hugged when they got one right. Whenever they got a question wrong, they banged on each other's backs and said, "Next time, buddy!"

I shook my head. "You know in real life they're thinking, 'What an idiot!'"

Gramps didn't say anything. The General lifted her leg and licked her butt, eyes steady on me.

I leaned forward and picked up my phone. Maybe I forgot to turn it off silent after karate and missed Dad's text. Nothing.

Tossing it back on the coffee table, I stretched out on the couch. It was nearly comfortable, until the nubby fabric brushed under my T-shirt. "Hey, did you hear about those cool new corduroy hats?" I asked.

Gramps grunted.

"Yeah," I said. "They're really making headlines."

Silence.

"Head . . . lines."

Silence.

Even though I was expecting it, the ding of my phone made me nearly jump out of my skin. Quicker than I thought possible for a geezer, Gramps swiped the phone off the table. He glared at it. "Just a picture of your girlfriend."

I yanked the phone out of his hand, half expecting a picture of Jocelyn. But it was Alice, making her dog Tooter wave a paw in my direction. I didn't bother replying, just dropped the phone back on the table.

"She's not my girlfriend," I muttered.

Gramps twisted away from me. "Who were you expecting?" he asked. On the television, a dad jumped up and down, wrapping his teenage son into a huge bear hug after correctly identifying the capital of Malta. (Valletta, for those of you playing along at home.)

I didn't answer.

"Your dad?" Gramps supplied anyway. He puffed noisily out of his nose and flicked his hand like he was shooing a bug. "What? He hasn't called you in a few days?" Still looking at the screen instead of me, he shook his head. "Been years, boy, since he called me. That is, 'til he needed something."

"Is that why you strike up conversations with the yard horse?" I asked, my voice hard and mean. The old man's hands fluttered up like I shocked him or something. I guess I had. "I'm sorry," I mumbled. "I just don't like you talking about my dad that way."

The old man nodded without looking at me and didn't say another word that night.

Chapter Twelve

Three months into the school year, and Gramps's '70s bungalow started to feel like home. I even adjusted to the idea of being a Papuaville Fighting Guinea Pig. I'd mastered going down the down stairs and up the up stairs at school. I hadn't caused bodily injury to Miss Singer in several weeks. And Jocelyn was still the rookie coach at Waters, which meant I never missed a practice. The only thing missing still: friends.

Now listen, I don't mean to brag much, but at Addison, making friends was not a problem. Even before Addison—before Artie—friends were never a problem. I'm what you might call charming. Flash of the dimple here, quick joke there, and *boom*. Friends. Maybe not known-you-forever friends, but buddies all the same.

Until, of course, I moved here.

Apparently when there's a hometown hero like Max and on your first day you manage to flirt with his girl *and* get him framed for bullying, as well as make a teacher pass out by popping out your own eyeball, then

get all whacked-out excited to be in quilting club, you're treated a bit like a freak.

I know, right? The injustice of it all is troubling.

Which makes moments like this one that I was in—gym class—oh so much fun.

Like I said before, I don't need a whole lot of special treatment because of my vision. I just need a front-row seat in the classroom, one that's to the right of the room so my left eye can take in the action. Papuaville Middle School does a lot of work on laptops and they had to special order one with a larger screen for me—fourteen inches instead of ten—but that's really it. Except for gym class. I'm supposed to be exempt from most sports with flying balls, since they're pretty much impossible for me to play. Only Mr. Chipps was one of those teachers who didn't actually read his paperwork. He was one of those teachers who had been at the job long enough to be beyond proving himself but not so jaded that he was trying to show up the other teachers by doing things like reading the forms detailing the accommodations I needed to compensate for Artie and the low vision in my real eye. He was in that happy, lazy medium. And I was one of those kids who sort of clung to the notion that I might actually have gotten better at gym class since last year. That maybe I didn't actually need those accommodations after all. That this year I could skip running laps during the tennis section and do push-ups during the dodgeball division.

So I never quite pointed out that I have a visual impairment.

Mr. Chipps's last section was badminton. The first couple classes, I just sort of hung out in the back. "Come on, now," Mr. Chipps had said. "Let's show some Guinea Pig pride! Just keep your eye on the birdy, son."

I thought at first he was joking. I almost congratulated him on the hilarious choice of phrasing.

"You just need some motivation," Mr. Chipps had said. "I'll put you with a stronger partner. Max Waters! You're with Richie Ryder."

Both of us groaned. "No way," said Lash Boy, throwing up his hands. "I'm already partners." He grabbed the kid closest to him, who turned out to be Marshall Lindstern. Let me just tell you, this was the first time Marshall Lindstern had been chosen as anyone's partner in as long as I've been in class. He squeaked a little in surprise.

Everyone around us took a huge step back from where I was standing. I checked quickly to make sure I wasn't showing signs of leprosy or foot-and-mouth disease. Nope, usual freckled skin and ginger hair. I sniffed casually at the pits. Still fresh. Yep. Dad could come home from Alaska any time and study middle school gym class for some insight into herd mentality: if Max didn't want to be my partner, neither did anyone else.

"Oh," Mr. Chipps said, as surprised as anyone—except maybe Marshall Lindstern—that the school's biggest, most competitive guy chose the skinniest, smallest kid to be his partner. "All right." He then jerked a thumb at Ryan Cashew.

Here's what you need to know about Ryan (how can I phrase this?): he was a jerk. A nearly six-foot-tall, box-shaped, slightly cone-headed kid whose internal radio station was constantly tuned to full volume. Everything he said was booming and angry.

"Are you kidding me?" Ryan yelled.

I plastered on my most aggravating grin and waved my fingertips at him. He shook his head like a dog shaking off a flea. I followed Ryan to our spot on the court, which was, of course, across the net from where Mr. Chipps had assigned Max and Marshall.

Then Ryan and Max kicked off a crazy, whole-court game while Marshall and I vaguely waved our rackets and tried not to get plowed over. All of this was great until we had to switch serves. Ryan totally freaked when I couldn't lob the stupid birdy over the net.

Max didn't say anything. Didn't even laugh along with Marshall as I threw up the birdy only to miss it entirely with the racket three times in a row. Finally, I managed to lob it over the net. Max deftly whapped it back.

"Are you even *trying*?" Ryan stormed when the birdy plopped me on the head. (Just to add to your mental picture here, let me tell you another injustice at this school: gym uniforMs. Maroon shorts about five inches too short and gray T-shirts with the school mascots plastered on them. Remember? The mascots are fighting guinea pigs. Just wanted you to be able to really picture me in all of my humiliation.)

"Dude, *one eye*," I snapped to Ryan, matching his volume. "Twenty-seventy vision. Remember?"

"Wait, what?" Mr. Chipps said. He stood in front of me, staring at my face. I almost felt sorry for the guy. I could practically see him mentally revisiting all the times he had said things like "Good eye!" and "Eye on the ball." Quietly, he whispered, "Do all the other teachers know about this?"

I nodded.

"Okay!" Mr. Chipps blew into his whistle six times. "Listen up, Guinea Pigs. We're going to spend the rest of class working on our skipping. Okay. So, um, power gallops and skips. All right? Go."

Great. We skipped like baby kindergarteners for a half-hour thanks to Artie.

That was last week. I hoped Mr. Chipps would be back to his regular curriculum this week. But when we got to class, Mr. Chipps motioned for us all to get back into the stupid skipping lines again.

"All right, Guinea Pigs." Mr. Chipps clapped his hands together heavily. "We're going to start a brand new section today. It's competitive. It's fast. And it's intense." He whistled slowly and then winked at me. I felt my hopes plummet, even as the rest of the guys cheered.

"That's right," Mr. Chipps said. "Today, we're all going to push ourselves." Too much emphasis on *all*.

Mr. Chipps held up a mesh bag. I was too far away to make out what was in the bag, but I heard a whole lot of grumbling and muttered curses from the other kids. "Competitive cup stacking!" Mr. Chipps upturned the bag, dumping dozens of plastic cups onto the gym floor, where they landed with a clatter.

Here's the thing: I know this whole competitive cup stacking is a pity sport. A let's-give-the-visually-impaired-kid-a-break move. But there are so many sports where I'm actually decent. Like track. And believe it or not, I'm also good at archery. (Side note: Did you know that many sharpshooters are one-eyed? I'm serious! Of course, their seeing eye is usually, you know, twenty-twenty. Still, I can hold my own with archery.) But cup stacking? If Mr. Chipps was looking to make everyone in this stupid school hate me, he was off to a fab start.

Worse yet, I was stuck stacking next to Lash Boy.

At first we both sort of just made pyramids. But I made mine a little faster. Then Lash Boy nabbed a couple cups rolling by from someone's destroyed pyramid, so his was a bit taller. I got a few more of my own and perfected letting them slip out of stack in rabid fire. *Pop, pop, pop.* Pyramid! Soon other guys were rolling theirs our way.

Max made a taller tower, but in the same time I made three smaller pyramids and dismantled them. "Okay, boys," said Mr. Chipps, holding a timer in his hand. "Now see who can be first to make three stacks of three."

I housed Lash Boy. A couple other guys whistled.

"Go, Ryder!" Marshall cheered.

Another guy I didn't know muttered, "Can't believe it, but this is actually kind of awesome."

"Now, one pyramid of three, one of ten, another pyramid of three. *Go!*"

Max finished his a half-second before me.

"Rematch," I muttered, pushing back my hair. Okay, so I was sweating. Whatever.

Even score, despite my useless glasses fogging.

"Again!" Lash Boy and I called at the same time. Someone even clapped, and Marshall hooted.

I flexed my fingers, hands hovering over my tower of cups. "A cycle this time," Mr. Chipps smirked. "First three, then ten, then three, then work backward. Another three, another ten, another three." He mimed piling the cups back into the single tower after each formation. "Got it?" he asked.

Lash Boy and I glared at each other. I took off my glasses and fixed my eye on the cups. "Ready," I said.

Lash Boy nodded.

"*Go!*"

We were off. For the first second, there was total silence, just the clapping of cups onto the gym floor. Then the guys started cheering. "Go, go, go!"

My hands were slick with sweat. Heart thumping. Pyramid up, cups stacked. Bigger pyramid, cups stacked again. Third pyramid up, stacked back down. Boom, back through the cycle. I didn't glance toward Max, even as I registered the sound of his towers. I was focused entirely on my towers. *Boom, boom, boom.*

"Done!" I shouted. Mr. Chipps pressed the timer.

Lash Boy had his hands still on his cups. My eyes swiveled to Mr. Chipps, making sure he registered my time.

Okay, here's the thing. When you have one eye, you've got to blink. Got to moisturize Artie, you know? If you don't—say when you're whopping somebody's butt in cup stacking and forget to blink—Artie gets dry. I rubbed at it, still moving in fast, jerky motions, and accidentally—*accidentally*—knocked Max's pyramid over with my elbow as I dismantled the last tower.

"Seriously?" Max yelled. "Cheater!"

Mr. Chipps shrugged. "Kid still won, regardless." He thumped me on the back as I rubbed Artie. A stream of tears leaked from the eye.

"Wow," someone whispered, "he's crying."

"Probably never won anything before," another answered.

"It's *discharge*!" I snapped. "From my eye!"

Max still grumbled. Just for sport, I threw up another couple towers while Max dismantled his.

"Whoa," a kid whispered to the other. "Maybe we should change our mascot to the Cyclops."

"Whatever," cone-headed Ryan Cashew grunted and kicked at my tower. "It's *cup stacking*, dude." Just like that, everyone snickered and headed to the locker room. Like I said, herd mentality.

Quilting club was the highlight of my week, another sign of serious trouble. All the other members spent the hour spilling deets about their lives. Honestly, I knew more about my fellow quilters than anyone else, aside from maybe Alice. I offered as much helpful advice as possible ("Janet May, God's honest truth here, no boy is going to appreciate the quilted tissue bag as much as you deserve."), which seemed to have opened me up to *getting* advice despite never sharing anything remotely personal. That is, until today when I blabbed about my cup-stacking superiority. Instead of cheering for me, they were standing up for Lash Boy.

"Look, you've got to give Max Waters a break," Janet May said as she waited patiently for me to thread her quilting needle. The club members make a big deal out of me threading their needles. I think it's because no one wants me working on their quilt squares. Apparently I have "sloppy stitches." Janet May nodded in approval when I knotted her thread.

"He's a sore loser," I said.

"Richie Ryder, he's a nice guy." Janet May loves double names, so I couldn't even slight her for using both my names. When someone doesn't have a double name, she just uses first and last names. Two braids went down the sides of her head to join into a ponytail, which she whipped back and forth. She was working on a double ring quilting patch.

I knew what Janet May was thinking—I had seen the photos on Instagram. Last week, she had a booth at a church craft fair. Janet May had been posting about it endlessly, asking people to come and "support the arts" and promising "custom, one-of-a-kind pieces." People started busting her in the comments. Someone asked if she could special order one of Janet May's quilted vests with teddy bears. The commenter said, "It'll go great when I borrow my mom's high-waisted jeans."

Here's the thing, though: Janet May didn't realize all the people "complimenting" her photo gallery of quilted wall hangings, coasters, and purses were making fun of her. She didn't know that the girl who left that comment was being mean. And Janet May made the teddy bear vest—even tagging the girl in the photo she posted.

Max was the only one who stopped it. He commented on Janet May's photo that the girl was a jerk. He said he'd see her at the fair. And you know what? He showed up. Janet May posted a photo of them. Suddenly, no one made fun of her anymore. The others deleted their comments. That's the way Lash Boy rolls. He's disgustingly decent.

I mean, I didn't comment or anything. I felt awful for Janet May. But I didn't stop it, either. I didn't do anything about it.

Suddenly, an image of Max in the hall, his arm around Jocelyn, flashed in my mind. Whatever. He might be nice, but he was still a jerk.

"Max is the reason no one will talk to me at this school," I pointed out.

"Maybe," Janet May said. "You know, I'd sit with you at lunch but I have my own crew."

"I know, Janet May. I know," I said. Say what you will about the quilting club, but they stick it to you straight. (You got that, didn't you?)

Next in line was Madelyn, whose natural hair color could rival Alice's for white-blond, but she had dyed it pitch black. Her coarse hair crinkled across her back as she moved like it was made of straw. While we had initially hit it off due to my all-black first-day wear and her all-black-all-the-time approach, we don't have a lot of similar interests. She liked to quilt dragons with teeth dripping blood on her quilt patches, for example. And I didn't quilt. I pretty much spent the hour threading needles.

"Well, you didn't know it when you moved here, but Max is, like, a god around here. He's a hero. He saved . . ." Madelyn's face flushed.

"Jocelyn," I said. "Yeah, I heard."

"Everyone has heard the story. Everyone knows Max. Everyone wants to be like Max. And you went and made him out to be a stupid bully on your very first day," Madelyn said.

"It was an accident," I mumbled around the thread in my mouth.

150

"Yeah, maybe. But you haven't stopped picking at him since! Stop blaming Max," Madelyn said. "It's *your* fault. You antagonize him all the time. Lay off him and just be yourself."

I let my gaze fall from her inky hair to the white pancake makeup coating her face to the black nail polish and huge combat boots. "Just be myself, huh?"

"Yeah," Madelyn said. "Just you, toned down a bit, maybe."

"How do you tone down being yourself?" I popped the thread through the needle eyehole and handed it to Madelyn.

"Well," said another quilt club friend, Jess, and then she sighed. Picture a mouse who overnight morphed into a fourteen-year-old girl. That's pretty much Jess. Squeaky voice and all. She spends all of quilting club piecing together tiny hammocks for real guinea pigs. "You could maybe not say *every* funny thought. Maybe forget a pun now and then."

"My thoughts are hilarious," I pointed out. "Everyone loves a pun."

Silence from the room. Miss Singer coughed into her elbow.

Janet May crossed her arMs. "Maybe if you spent less time trying to make Max Waters look silly and everyone else laugh, you'd have someone to sit with in the cafeteria."

"Seriously? You guys need to develop a sense of humor. Maybe all of these synthetic fabrics have rotted yours." I tossed an empty spool into the trashcan, missing spectacularly. "My self-esteem is hanging on by a thread here."

The quilt club let out a collective groan.

"I'm sorry," Madelyn said. "You're just not nearly as funny as you think you are."

"That's ridiculous."

Silence.

Miss Singer cleared her throat again. "Richie Ryder, I want to try a little experiment. Bear with me a second."

"Uh, I don't know . . ." I said, looking around at the club members. I knew they had been talking about me behind my back.

"I suspect," Miss Singer said, "that you are a gifted observer of what goes on around you."

"Very funny." I fake laughed.

Miss Singer shook her hands in front of her. "I'm not referring to your vision, Richie Ryder. I'm referring to what goes on around you. For example, tell me, what do you know about Jess? This is a safe place and I know you'll be kind," she added when both Jess and I gaped. "Simply tell me what you've learned about her in the few weeks you've been with us."

Confused, I blurted, "Quilt club was her first pick of experientials. She has more school pride than anyone in the history of time, despite our mascot. Or maybe because of it. Jess has five guinea pigs and hasn't told her parents yet that she's pretty sure Hester is actually a Henry and soon they will have many, many guinea piglets." Jess's face flushed as I added, "She has a crush on Georgie Wilson and dreams of one day owning an alpaca farm."

"It's true," Jess said. "I love alpacas."

"And Madelyn?" Miss Singer asked.

Automatically I replied, "She claims to love emo eighties bands but hums nineties boy band hits when she quilts. She smells like vanilla because she bakes cookies for her little brother and sister after school. Madelyn uses scotch tape to fix bent flowers in the courtyard."

Madelyn sucked in her breath. "I do *not* like the Backstreet Boys."

"Yeah, but you *love* *NSYNC. *This I Promise You*," I sing-songed. Madelyn rolled her eyes.

"Janet May?" Miss Singer prompted. I glanced at the girl, whose eyes widened and cheeks flushed.

"Janet May got a double dose of honesty and is the one you go to if you want to know if you've got spinach stuck in your teeth or if the cat hair on your pants is noticeable. She is not the one to go to if you want to hear that you're right in an argument."

Janet May shrugged. The other girls nodded.

"And me?" Miss Singer asked softly.

I bit my lip, still not knowing where this was headed. "You think about your students all the time, years after they leave your classroom. You love biology but can't stand blood, which makes it really hard to be the quilting teacher, where—before yours truly and his awesome one-eyed-needle-threading powerhouse talent—you routinely stabbed yourself in the thumb. In fact, I'm pretty sure you hate quilting, given how I have yet to see you keep a stitch. I think you only took on the job because if you didn't, there wouldn't be a quilting club and you like getting to know us more than you like teaching us."

Miss Singer nodded. She got up from her seat, the sound of her chair pushing back against the cement floor echoing in the loud silence of the room. When she kneeled in front of me, her hand squeezing my shoulder, she looked me straight in the face. Her green eyes flicked back and forth across my eyes, finally steadily staring at the one that could stare back. Even though she was watching me, she addressed the rest of the club. "Okay, ladies. Your turn. Aside from the fact that he has a visual impairment and a fondness for puns, what do you know about Richie Ryder?"

No one spoke. Janet May opened and closed her mouth like a guppy then quietly shook her head. Madelyn scratched at the nail polish on her thumb. Jess rolled her lips nervously.

"Maybe what I'm trying to say sounds harsh," Miss Singer added. She folded her hands and rested her chin on them. "It *is* harsh. But look at all you've learned from us, Richie. You deserve the same in a friendship. Any relationship you want will only work if you show up, too. I don't think anyone really knows you. They know you'll make them laugh—or roll their eyes. But that's all you share. We don't actually *know* you."

I felt something boil inside me, starting in my feet, which suddenly drummed against the ground. My knees jerked up and down. The churning bubbled up my gut, gushing into my chest, across my shoulders, and down my arms to my fingertips. Like a wave crashing into a bucket, it filled my head. My eyes—yes, both—stung from the inside out.

This storm raged in me, and I knew that if I opened my mouth it would erupt, scalding Miss Singer and melting down the whole room. This whole stupid, joke-in-it-self quilting club filled with stupid losers who thought they had a right to talk about me. To judge *me*. Whatever. I ground my teeth together to keep the unfamiliar rage inside.

A nasty voice in my head whispered that the rage wasn't really all that unfamiliar. It had simmered from the first moment I saw my seven-year-old self with a bandage over one eye. It had boiled to the surface whenever

I saw Max with Jocelyn. It was what made my voice edgy and mean when Gramps confronted me about Dad. It was always quietly bubbling away. Usually, though, it was easier to squash with a witty comeback.

Squeezing my shoulder again, Miss Singer said softly, "Richie, all we know about you is that you're someone who jokes around."

Janet May stood and moved just behind Miss Singer. "When you turn everything into a joke, Richie Ryder, you *become* the joke. Is that what you want?"

I felt my nostrils flare as I fought for a steady breath. I wouldn't wipe at my eyes but there was no way I was letting one of those tears fall, either. I never cried. Never. Didn't cry when I lost an eye. Didn't cry before that when Mom wanted a "normal" picture of me. Didn't cry when my dad picked watching freaking buffalos over living with his kid. So there was no way I would cry now.

Something about the way Miss Singer blinked at me, her eyes wide and watching for my reaction, made me think about when I was a little kid, still wearing a patch over what would soon be Artie, sitting in front of Therapy Panda as he prattled on and on about it being okay to feel however I felt. And deciding that I was only going to feel happy from then on.

I felt the wave pull back. I swallowed down the thick emotion, pushing it to wherever it had escaped like a geyser. *No.* I smiled, even though it felt nasty on my face.

"Is this some sort of quilt club intervention?" I asked.

"That depends," Miss Singer said, still in her Therapy Panda voice. "How'd we do?"

"Sew, sew," I said, grabbing my backpack and letting the door slam behind me before they could figure out the joke.

Chapter Thirteen

"Whoa," Jocelyn said that night at Waters Martial Arts. "You're fired up tonight."

I shrugged.

"Everything okay?"

I didn't answer, just punched the targets a bit faster. Jocelyn didn't push for details. A side effect of having no social life—and, fine, also having an enormous crush on the instructor—made me a model student. I usually joked around between forms with the other students, but nothing seemed all that funny tonight. Maybe it was because Gramps was watching from the sidelines. Things had been a little awkward between us ever since I let him know I heard him talking to the yard horse. I guess that's why I asked him if he wanted to come in and watch class tonight. "I'll stay for a minute or two," he had said. "Your mom's going to pick you up. It's free donut night for seniors at the Stop N Shop, so I can't miss that."

Jocelyn had been teaching us forms, calling out cues for each move. Anyone who messed up a step or

159

couldn't keep up had to sit down on the mat. Soon, I was the only one standing. Jocelyn called out cues faster and faster, but I didn't miss a single move. I glanced over at Gramps when Jocelyn turned to straighten her belt. He gave me a thumbs up before heading out to his Goldsmobile to leave for his free donut.

My "reward" was target hitting. Jocelyn put a younger black belt—Peggy, the ten-year-old with pigtails of fury—in charge of the rest of the group, running them through the forms again and again. Meanwhile, Jocelyn picked up the handheld targets to work on punching and kicking with me. At the last class, Master Waters said I was inches away from sparring for real.

"You're doing really well," Jocelyn said.

The door swung open, letting in a blast of cold air. I didn't turn from the target but watched Jocelyn's face change when her eyes slid to the door. Her mouth twitched into a quick smile. Max.

I punched a little harder, kicked a little faster. Jocelyn's smile now was turned on me. "Add in a side-step." She mimed the move, throwing out a roundhouse kick for me to dodge, then holding up the target for a jab, twisting it out for my side kick. My moves were dodge, jab, side kick. Dodge, jab, side kick.

"Faster!" she ordered. Everything else—even Max and the other guys watching from the mat—faded

away. (Mostly.) *Dodge, jab, side kick. Dodge, jab, side kick.*
Dodgejabsidekick.

Only I guess I went too fast because a side kick actually did hit Jocelyn, knocking her just above the belt and
pushing her back a foot.

"I'm sorry! I'm sorry!" I yelped as she fell back on
her butt.

"Don't be sorry! That was awesome!" Jocelyn grinned.

Master Waters strode forward and held out his
hand for Jocelyn, hoisting her to her feet. Everyone on
the mat—and everyone waiting for the advanced class,
including Max—seemed to be holding their breath. No
one spoke. Turning back to me, Master Waters said,
"Good skill set, but can you fight when the target fights
back?"

I nodded. "I think so, sir."

"Are you serious?" Jocelyn asked. "Am I finally off
rookie duty?"

Master Waters crossed his beefy arMs. "How about
you stick around after your regular class for sparring
next week," he said to me.

"Yes, sir."

Jocelyn bounced on the balls of her feet. I grinned at
her and she clapped her hands.

"Does this mean I get to take class tonight instead of
just teaching the rookies?" Jocelyn asked Master Waters.

"Suppose so," he said.

"Finally!" Jocelyn darted to the edge of the mat, where Max whirled her around in a circle.

"Sparring drills!" Master Waters called to the class, who let out a cheer. Jocelyn knelt by her duffel bag, putting on her sparring gear.

Master Waters blocked my view of Jocelyn, stepping directly in front of me. "We have a sparring class on Monday between the beginners and advanced classes. Don't think for a minute that sparring means you stop taking regular classes. You need to do both to be part of the team." I nodded and Master Waters added that he needed a note from my homeroom teacher, verifying my grades were decent and my effort in class good.

"Just so I can fight?" I asked.

Master Waters nailed me with a glare so sharp it could've skewered one of Mom's bugs. "Waters Martial Arts is known as a premier fighting school. No one beats us." He gestured to the trophies lining the room. "The reason no one beats us is because of our unparalleled expectations for students. You will be successful on the mat, and you will carry that success off the mat in school and in your personal life."

I bit back my urge to look over my shoulder for a camera crew. Clearly this speech was meant for commercials—or at minimum had been delivered in front of the mirror dozens of times. Given the fact that earlier today I discovered not everyone appreciates my finely tuned sense of humor, combined with the fact that this man could probably do some ninja trick that replaced my face with my butt, I opted to simply nod. "Yes, sir," I added, when the skewer look didn't soften.

Master Waters nodded. "I'll make sure you have a set of sparring gear ready by Monday. Do you need to wear those glasses?"

I nodded. "Mom'll flip if I don't. They protect my good eye."

"Most kids who wear glasses try to get contacts for sparring."

"That won't work for me," I snapped. Master Waters's eyes widened. "Sir," I added hastily.

Master Waters mashed his lips together. "I think I have a helmet with a face shield in the back somewhere. Wearing it'll be tricky as it affects depth perception, but then you won't have to wear the glasses underneath. They'll fog up fast."

I nodded, trying to feel excited to be in sparring. I mean, I *was* excited, about three seconds ago when Jocelyn was cheering. But then I thought she was cheering because I had done such an awesome job. But, no. She was cheering to be rid of instructing me!

Like he could read my storming thoughts, Max walked by, fake punching me in the shoulder with his padded-up hand. "Thanks, man," he said around his mouth guard. "Glad to have my girlfriend back again."

I didn't say anything, just shrugged.

"And already looking forward to Monday's fight," he added in an undertone as his dad walked off.

I slowly left the mat and took a seat in the chairs lined up along the wall for moms and dads. Mom was already twenty minutes late. I texted her about ten minutes later, tired of watching Max maneuvering to be next to Jocelyn in line. Tired of him glancing over to make sure I saw, too.

Mom, where are you?

A minute later, she replied.

Sorry, Ryder! Had to find a good place to pull over and respond. In traffic. Be there in ten.

But ten minutes later, the advanced class was over and Mom still wasn't there.

Max grabbed a giant broom and swept down the mats. Jocelyn pulled targets to the corners of the room. Master Waters turned off lights in the changing rooms and bathrooMs. I pretended to be invisible. Can you picture the awkwardness? The three of them shutting down the place; me just sitting there. I thought about asking what I could do to help, but it'd be oh so much more

164

awkward when they finished the clean-up routine even earlier thanks to my help and Mom *still* wasn't there. So I just sat there, staring at the phone on my lap, wishing Gramps had a cell phone so I could pull him away from his jelly-filled treat to come and get me.

I would've waited outside but it started raining (of course) and was just barely above freezing.

Eventually, Master Waters stood in front of me. "Do you need to borrow a phone to call your mom?" he asked, even though I was, in fact, holding my phone.

"She's on her way, commuting from DC and stuck in traffic."

Master Waters nodded and crossed his arMs. He was too far away to confirm this, but I think the squeaking sound I heard was his teeth gnashing.

"I can wait outside," I said. "There's a coffee shop across the street. I'll text her to pick me up there, instead."

"Great," Max said. "Let's go." He put his arm around Jocelyn. I could feel her watching me but didn't look her way.

"Don't be ridiculous," she said. I did look then and saw her shrug off Max's arm. "Master Waters, Ryder lives next door to me." She turned toward me for a second. "Can you just give him a lift, too?"

"Don't you and Max want to head to our house for some grub like you usually do?" Master Waters asked.

"I have a lot of homework," Jocelyn said. "I'd rather just go home tonight." Two bright red splotches appeared on Max's face. I worked very, very hard on not smiling.

"All right." Master Waters opened the door. "Let's go."

We ran from the school to Master Waters's Jeep, the rain blasting against our heads. The air was so bitter I had to fight not to shiver, though my teeth did clack together slightly. Artie gets cold fast, and I felt streaks of heat down my cheek as tears joined the raindrops on my face.

Jocelyn hopped in the back of Master Waters's Jeep and Max pushed me backward with his shoulder to slide in next to her. "Sit up with me, son," Master Waters said to Max. "You're not going to want to switch seats when we drop these two off at the same spot in this rain."

This time I didn't bother to hide my smile. I let it loose right in Lash Boy's furious face. His nostrils flared.

"Come on!" said Jocelyn, interrupting our stare off. "It's cold." I slid into the seat next to her and pulled out a bottle of eyedrops from my duffel bag. When Artie starts tearing up, a few drops usually get things back to normal. I didn't want it to look like I was crying or something because Mom wasn't there. Master Waters, Max, and Jocelyn suddenly all seemed very preoccupied with their seatbelts.

"It's just eyedrops," I said. "I'm not taking it out or anything."

"Does—can you go in the rain?" Max stuttered.

"Yeah, I only take it out every couple of months. It's just the cold, not the rain, that's bothering me." Lash Boy's mouth dropped open, and I knew another question he didn't want to ask and I didn't want to answer was about to trickle out. Sometimes I wished I had a FAQ sheet to distribute to answer questions such as: *Can you sleep in it?* Yes. *Can you swim with it?* Yes. *Can I hold it?* No.

Max sucked on his lip. His cheeks flushed red for a moment. "I didn't mean to—"

"Nah, don't sweat it," I said. Maybe it was the lashes, but sometimes it was actually tough to be mad at the guy. He was so freaking nice, you know?

Just then, yellow lights lit up the inside of the car. Mom's station wagon pulled up behind us. She beeped in two quick bursts.

"Isn't that your mom's car?" Jocelyn prodded when I didn't move.

"Perfect timing, as usual." I slipped out of the seat, grabbing my duffel bag. "Thank you anyway, Master Waters."

"Hang on a sec, son," he said, and opened the glove box. He rummaged for a second and pulled out a

167

brochure while the rain drummed against the back of my neck. Master Waters handed me the paper. "Give this to your mom. It has our schedule printed, so she remembers when to pick you up."

I stood there a second too long, almost ready to spout out that it didn't matter if he tattooed the time on Mom's forehead. If she—or Dad, if we're being honest—got caught up in research, nothing else mattered. Not eating, not other commitments, certainly not pickup times. But I didn't even make a joke. I just closed the door.

Mom's apologies pelted me faster than the rain as I got into the station wagon. "Oh, Ryder! Traffic was awful! If I had known that two more minutes in the lab would mean forty more in traffic, I'd never have done it." But then her voice rose to buzzing hum. "But, Ryder! We're so, so close to determining the temperature threshold for insect development. The possibilities this implies, especially for emerging mosquito populations . . ."

On and on she droned, not even noticing when I slipped on earbuds.

Late that night, the rain stopped. It ended so suddenly it was like a door slamming shut. One second rain bulleted against the windows of my bedroom. The next, silence. Sleep was just out of my reach anyway, but impossible in the sudden quiet.

I crept out of the bedroom, not turning on any lights. My head was such a mess—a karate-chopping, cup-stacking, girl-crushing mess. I used my newbie ninja skills to be super quiet so Mom and Gramps wouldn't wake up and ask me what I was doing. I just might've told them the truth when what I really needed was to figure out a way to push it all aside and clear my head again.

I grabbed a sweatshirt and pulled it on as I opened the front door. I wondered if I'd be able to see the stars now that the storm had cleared. Stars are something I remember from before. We'd go camping a lot on weekends, and I remember Dad pointing out the constellations and Mom turning them into stories. I used to be able to spot the Bear no matter where I was. But now, it was trickier. Twenty-seventy vision doesn't affect me too much, but I do miss seeing the stars well. The only time I could really make out constellations was in Montana last year. There, the stars were so bright I think Artie could've made them out.

When I looked up at the night sky, all I saw were shades of gray and black. If the stars were out, I couldn't see them. I sighed through my nose and leaned against the yard horse (which was holding a pumpkin and wearing devil horns).

"Trouble sleeping?"

For a heart-clenching second I thought the yard horse was talking to me! (That certainly would shed a new light on Gramps's conversations with it.) Even more startling, the voice came from the horse's behind. "I couldn't sleep, either."

By then I figured out who was speaking, though she was on my blind side. Even so, I said, "Well, that's because you're a cement horse."

"*Har har.*" Jocelyn stepped around the horse toward me. "Insomniac?" she asked.

"It got quiet," I said by way of explanation.

Jocelyn nodded. "I hate rain," she said. "I could probably fall asleep now; I had to make sure it really stopped."

I arched an eyebrow, waiting for her to explain why she hated the rain. But she didn't say anything, just stared up at the sky. "It's so beautiful, isn't it?"

I didn't bother looking up again. "Yeah."

"So," Jocelyn said, her face still upturned, "your mom."

I sighed. "She gets caught up in things."

"Are you okay?" Jocelyn asked. She took a half step closer to me so that now I felt her hair tickle my cheek.

"Why wouldn't I be?"

"No reason." Jocelyn turned toward me, her breath a warm cloud by my ear. For a second I thought, *if I turned toward her . . . if I leaned in . . .* But quick as a clap, Jocelyn turned away. "Good night, Richie Ryder. Enjoy the stars."

"Good night," I whispered as she disappeared into the dark on my right.

Chapter Fourteen

I guess I eventually fell asleep after going back to bed, because suddenly daylight streamed in through my windows. For a minute I had that oh-crap-what-time-is-it panic that always comes along with waking up with too much sun on my face on a Saturday morning. Then I did the most reasonable thing: just rolled on my left side so my working eye was covered with my pillow and tried to fall back asleep.

"*Cah, cah, cah!*"

No such luck. Gramps was busting a gut about something in the kitchen. Even folding the pillow up over my ears wouldn't block out the guffaws. I heard a second voice, though, definitely male. I popped up out of the bed, falling to the floor with a thud when the blankets swirled and tightened around my legs. Kicking them off, I shot to the door, throwing it open and rushing down the hall.

"Dad?" I called, sleep falling too slowly from me to remember to sidestep the General. She was in her usual

spot at the end of the hall, ready to pounce. Which she did, wrapping her mean yellow paws around my leg and sinking her teeth into my calf.

I heard the chairs slide back on the linoleum floor. "Richie Ryder," Gramps called, "it's—"

"Dad?" I called again. I rushed into the kitchen, sliding in my socks, and finding myself face to face with Logan. (Don't remember Logan? He was the skinny, ruddy-faced kid with floppy brown hair whose chair I stole on my first day of school. He'd given me the stink-eye every day since. Line up all the people who hated me at Papuaville Middle School and Logan and Max would pummel each other to be first.)

"Logan," Gramps finished. He tilted his head toward me. "Logan, this is my grandson, Richie Ryder."

"We've met," I said before Logan could reply. "What are you doing here?" I scraped off the General with my other ankle and covered my nether-regions with my hands. Did I mention that I was just wearing boxers and socks?

Logan didn't seem to know where to look. His mouth hung open. Eventually, he sat down and stared at Gramps.

"Let's just get on with the interview." Gramps sighed.

"Interview?" I said, pushing the General away a little farther with my foot. She hissed at me and slowly licked her leg while still glaring.

In a why-are-you-still-here tone, Gramps said, "Logan here is a Boy Scout. Interviewing me for a service project so he can earn his Eagle award."

"You're the service project? Is it, like, an expose on why people have things like yard horses?"

Gramps turned his back to me. Logan piped up, still not looking at me, "I'm working on promoting a center for people who've lost a family member. Widows, widowers, and kids. I'm interviewing people to find out what they need most."

"Oh," I said. Because what else could I say, standing there in my underpants while the kid I dismissed as a loser reveals he's doing something fantastic for the community. Then I had another thought: Jocelyn. "Are you interviewing him about Jocelyn's brother?"

Logan's face shot to me, but he clearly remembered I was almost naked and his eyes flipped back to Gramps. "No."

Gramps sighed again. "No, idiot. He's interviewing *me*. A widower."

Logan cleared his throat. "I got names from the senior center. That's how I heard about Mr. Raymond."

"Oh." I just stood there like . . . well . . . an idiot. A self-centered idiot who didn't remember for a second that his own grandma was dead. "I'm going to go get dressed."

"You do that," Gramps said. Logan puffed air through his cheeks in apparent relief.

A few minutes later, I walked oh-so-casually down the hall wearing actual pants. My plan was to grab a granola bar and seize control of the TV while Logan occupied Gramps. Instead, by the time I was where the hallway met the kitchen, I found myself leaning with my back against the wall, listening to the old man.

". . . met her when I was about seventeen, married less than a year later." I heard a creak as Gramps leaned back in the kitchen chair and also the scribble of Logan's pencil across his notebook.

"Why get married right away?" Logan asked. "I mean, you were so young."

"*Cah, cah, cah*! Young fools, I guess." Then Gramps's voice dipped, the words trickling out in the pause of Logan scribbling notes. "She had this laugh, you know? One that was only for me, when I was the one doing something she thought was funny. That laugh—I'd do anything to hear it."

There was a pause and the flipping of pages. I guess Logan was looking for his next question. But Gramps added, words gushing faster, "Good thing, too, that it was darned easy to make her laugh. I mean it. She'd laugh at just about anything I'd say or do. Funny faces, stupid jokes. The sillier the better." He laughed softly, and then his words rushed out, "You should've heard her when I got a whoopee cushion under her seat at the movies on our third date! She giggled through the whole movie. By the end of the film, I knew that was it. She was mine."

What was her laugh like? I wanted to know. But Logan didn't ask, so I didn't know if it was soft and rippling, like the sheets Mom would hang to dry in the sun when we were camping, or if it was loud and popping, like a balloon bursting. Or was it a laugh mostly felt in her eyes, the way Jocelyn's narrowed and tilted upward when I did something funny?

"So," Logan said, "you married her so you could make her laugh?"

"People marry for stupider reasons all the time, kid." Gramps sighed. "'Sides, Marlene, she didn't have such a great life. Lived in a foster home, you know. Not a lot of love there. When she turned eighteen, she'd be on her own anyway. Sort of made it my job to make her happy . . ." Again I heard Gramps shift in his chair. Quickly, like he was swallowing medicine, he added, "To make up for all of that. To give her all the love she lost growing up, and then some."

For some stupid reason, that made me think of Max.

"But you don't want to hear all about that," Gramps said.

"Actually—" Logan started, but Gramps cleared his throat, cutting Logan off.

I peeked around the corner. Logan, sitting facing me, gaped but didn't say anything, just shook his head slightly. Gramps sat with his back mostly toward me in the cramped kitchen, but I could see his profile. His lips were pursed, like a dam blocking in his memories. Soon enough, the dam burst. "We got married," he said as Logan scribbled in his notepad. "Wish you could've seen her face a few years later, when we got this here house."

"She was excited?" Logan asked.

"Spent hours pulling furniture into place, only to move it all an hour or so later, maybe even to another room. Putting a vase just so on the corner of a table. Adding flowers here, taking down a picture there. Always fixing it up. Made it into a show house."

Sure enough, Logan was scanning the house, no doubt noticing that it looked like nothing had changed at all in about forty years.

"I don't have an eye for that stuff," Gramps said lightly.

"Huh. Now, when was your son born?"

"Nineteen-seventy-six."

"Same year your wife died?" Logan flipped pages of his notes, like he was searching to make sure he hadn't messed up and written the wrong year.

"Same day," Gramps said softly. My throat felt too tight suddenly. I knew Dad's mom died from cancer when he was a baby. I hadn't realized it was the day he was born.

"Did she die in childbirth? The profile you filled out said she had cancer." More rustling paper.

Gramps leaked out a long, low breath. "I guess you could say she died of both. Found out she had breast cancer about two months into her pregnancy. The docs all said to end the pregnancy. To live, get treatment, and try to have another baby. But Marlene, well, by then we had heard the little heartbeat. Her own heart . . ." Gramps sucked in more air. "I think it's sort of like she grew an extra heart along with that little body growing inside her, a heart that just was his. Totally his."

"Did you . . ." Logan's voice was shaking a little. "Did you want her to end the pregnancy, too?"

"Didn't matter what I wanted." Gramps sort of laughed. "I knew better than to try and argue with her. I don't think I really knew how sick she was, either, 'til it was too late."

Logan didn't say anything for a minute. Gramps shuffled in his seat. "Even when docs said she should have the baby early, that he'd likely survive and she'd have a shot at living a few months or a year, she refused. Was so sick, in so much pain she couldn't hardly move."

"Why—"

"She was determined that the baby make it even if she couldn't stick around to meet him proper. Marlene parked herself in that recliner in there, facing out the window, watching the neighbor kids playing. Sometimes that'd make her smile and she'd say, 'Richie, promise me. You promise me that our boy will laugh and play, no matter what.'"

Logan's pencil stopped. "You know, Mr. Raymond, I didn't mean to pry here. I just wanted some general information. If you don't want to talk about this—"

"If I didn't want to talk, I wouldn't talk," Gramps said, his voice cold. A slurp of coffee later, he added, "Today's the anniversary, you know. Guess I'm a little sentimental. Plus, been decades since anyone asked me about her."

"Anniversary? Of when she passed?" Logan asked.

"No, of when she was diagnosed."

"Oh."

Shifting again, Gramps's crowing laughter rippled across the room to where I crouched in the hallway. "You know how I found out? I mean, about it being terminal?"

"How?" Logan asked, but in a way that sounded a lot like he'd rather not know.

"I come home to find her on the phone, calling horse farms all over town trying to find someone willing to let a pregnant, dying woman ride a horse. *Cah, cah, cah!*"

"What?" Logan asked, or maybe it was me.

180

"She's sitting there, crying that she never got to have a horse. Over the years, you know, she had told me she loved horses. Said it was her Christmas wish every year. Wanted to ride one of her own someday. I thought it was just a fantasy. A joke, you know? I worked at the factory. Buying this house, it wiped out any savings we had. Add to it the cost of her treatments, what it took to take care of the baby . . . well, that was that."

"Is that why you have the thing out front?"

"The yard horse?" Gramps asked in his casual, of-course-it's-a-yard-horse tone.

"Um, yeah."

"I took over making calls for Marlene. Found this guy, this horse farm owner, who said he's moving to Florida, just got rid of all his horses. Says the only thing left was a five-foot-tall stone horse. I said, 'I'll take it.' Got it delivered, set it up to be right outside her window. Even dressed it up for her, with flowers and chocolates." I could hear the smile in his voice as he added, "Wish you could've heard her laugh."

Soft. Rippling. That's how I heard it.

"Toward the end, she'd rub that big belly—looked so strange to see a body swelling like that while the rest of her faded away—and talk to the baby. 'Bout our lives. Telling him how much she loved him. How much I loved him."

"Did you, though? Love him, I mean." Logan cleared his throat. "I bet it was difficult."

Gramps laughed, a strangled, rattling, broken chuckle. "By the end, I did. When I realized he was the only thing keeping her hanging on—not me, not some stupid yard horse, not anything. When she was too weak to talk to the baby, I would, my hand on her stomach. I told him I'd make sure he'd know her—always be surrounded by her—the way the baby was then."

I let my eyes wander around the house again, knowing now why Gramps wouldn't so much as move a picture from an end table. I didn't even lie to myself and say the wetness on my cheeks was Artie acting up.

"I loved the kid. 'Course I did. But the day he was born was the day she left. New love here, old love gone. Just gone. And Marlene did her best—lasted longer than anyone thought—trying to give Tom a healthy start. But he was born a little too soon. A little too weak. Almost lost him, too."

Logan coughed, like he was trying to change the topic, but Gramps kept barreling on.

"Can you imagine? Asking the funeral director to hold on a few days, in case we needed to bury a baby, too?" Gramps's voice strained, became high-pitched. "After I knew he'd make it, I tried to show him I loved him the way I had shown her—by making him laugh, being silly—

but every time I saw him, I saw her, too." He sighed again. "Think I could've done a better job of hiding that."

I realized then that I wasn't crying for Gramps. I was crying for my dad, never knowing his mom, never really knowing his father, either. I covered my mouth with my hands, trying to stay silent.

"Well," Logan said after a pause, "part of this project is finding ways to help people sort of move on after someone they love dies. How did you move on?"

A long, thick pause blanketed the room. "I kept going on, you know?" I heard Gramps's chair push back, his heavy footsteps as he moved to the sink. The water turned on and he must've been rinsing out his coffee cup. My ankles were burning from crouching so long but I couldn't get up yet. I needed to hear what he said next. "Took care of our boy, you know?"

He moved back to the chair and settled in. "Marlene, her last words were, 'Keep laughing.' Can you imagine that? I try to do that, to make everyone laugh." My mind flashed images—Gramps buzzing me with his handshake shocker, flirting with the school office ladies, signing me up for quilting. All the things that annoyed the crap out of me.

Logan didn't say anything for a long time. Then he cleared his throat and said, "No, um. I guess the question wasn't clear. I was wondering how you moved on?"

"Well, I keep her memory alive. I dress up the horse, you see, in case it makes anyone else laugh like she did. Keep the house the way she liked it."

"But—"

I got up before Logan could press the question again. "Am I like her at all?" I asked, entering the kitchen.

Gramps's eyes widened as I burst into the room. He scanned me, from toes to head. "You have her eye."

I know, I know. It's a terrible joke. Not even funny, and I would've delivered it a thousand times better. But I snorted, then couldn't stop laughing, especially when I saw how totally uncomfortable Logan was, his eyes twisting between Gramps and me.

In fact, I didn't pull myself together until after Logan had gathered up his notebook and pencil, said an awkward bye, and left (but first Gramps thanked him for stopping by, adding, "Wish I had a grandson like you.").

"I mean it," I said, the click of the screen door shutting acting like a period to my sentence. "Am I like her?"

"You have her laugh, too, I guess." Gramps smiled down at his hands.

Loud. Popping. Now I knew exactly what she sounded like.

Alice FaceTime pinged me three times before I answered.

"Why are you dodging me?" she asked, her eyes darting as she held the screen. She has a habit of holding the screen way too close to her face when she's nervous or upset, so I only saw her eyes.

"Back up, Porcelain," I mumbled. "I'm not dodging you."

Alice cocked an eyebrow.

"All right. Maybe I'm dodging you a little. I have a lot on my mind."

"Like what?" she asked. She put the iPad on the table for a second and picked up Tooter. The dog snorted and licked at her chin, then put its head on her shoulder in a limp sort of way.

"How is he?" I asked. More than a year ago, Tooter had been diagnosed with a brain tumor. It was slower growing than the vet had originally thought, but I knew—and Alice knew—the pup was on borrowed time.

Alice burrowed her cheek against Tooter's side. "Won't be long now. In fact . . ." she shifted a little and moved a towel under Tooter. "He pees on us all the time."

This uplifting little chat wasn't really helping with the I'm-such-an-idiot feeling. "Look, doll, I've got to go."

"*Ryder*," Alice scolded. "What's going on?"

Alice had this strange ability to make everyone share their life stories with her even when they didn't want to.

I've seen it in action many times. In fact, she won this huge town essay contest because of it. Anyway, I found myself whispering, "I'm a jerk."

"You're not a jerk."

"I am. I'm a jerk." I squeezed shut my eyes and just blurted, "I thought Gramps was pathetic when he's really just lonely. I picked a fight with probably the nicest guy in the whole school. I'm jealous that my parents love each other more than they love me. I hate looking at myself in the mirror. And—prepare yourself, Porcelain—I'm not funny."

Alice burst out laughing.

"No, you misheard. I'm not funny."

Alice bit down her laughter. "You're rambling, Ryder. Slow down. What's the first thing you said—about Gramps?"

I opened my eyes. I saw my best friend, sitting there, holding her dying dog, and looking at me with nothing but interest. Nothing but a feeling of wanting to help. Like what I had to say was worth hearing. Worth working out. I looked away. One thing you should know about Alice: she always tells the truth, even if you don't want to hear it.

Sucking in a lungful of air, I grinned. "Great chat, Alice! Feel better now. See you later." I hung up before she could reply.

Chapter Fifteen

ere's a joke for you: What's five foot six, one hundred and fifteen pounds, and completely clueless about life?

I'll let you ponder that for a minute.

My head started pounding the minute I woke up Monday morning. I thought about telling Mom, but I knew if I stayed home from school there would be no way she'd let me go to sparring, and I didn't want to miss my first day. Instead, I swallowed two (okay, three) Advil.

It worked for a while, but by my second class, it felt like this little old man had moved into my skull and kept rearranging furniture. *It's just from not sleeping much,* I told myself.

All this self-deprecation I had been wallowing in had seriously affected my ability to keep up with homework. I had spent hours reading *Angela's Ashes,* falling asleep with it covering my face and dreaming about the River Shannon, only it was filled with eyeballs.

187

I told the little old man to flatten the bit of my brain that kept wondering if this headache was like the headaches I had when I was a kid, before Artie.

Making my way to history class, I didn't even try to count the doors. If I didn't find the door on the first try, I'd just keep walking. But there was a bright green strip of duct tape covering the doorframe of one room. I had noticed the same green strip outside Miss Singer's class in biology, which I chalked up to her upcoming frog dissection (she had been decking out everything in the room green for the occasion). I stopped and walked in. Sure enough, it was history. There was Max sitting in his usual spot right by the door.

Have you ever seen someone actively trying *not* to notice you? Like looking literally everywhere in the room but at you, even though you're literally in front of him? That was Max in this moment. His backpack was open at his feet. There was a roll of electric green duct tape hanging out from it.

"That was your doing?" I asked, thumbing toward the doorway.

Max, still not looking at me, shrugged.

"Why?" I asked. I mean, the guy hated me, right?

"Does it help?" he asked.

I nodded. "Yeah, man. It helps a lot."

Max shrugged again. "That's why."

And there you have it—the answer to the non-joke above.

Me.

I was a giant marshmallow.

While more advanced Waters Martial Arts fighters had black sparring suits, I was still in my white uniform. Add to that white foam feet protectors and white foam gloves. The foam helmet—also white—had a clear face shield, which, thankfully, blurred some of the other fighters' reaction to see they were about to take on the Stay Puft Marshmallow Man.

Master Waters tightened the straps on my helmet. "All right, son," he said. "One thing missing." Then he unknotted the white belt cinching my waist. He handed me a folded-up yellow belt, bowing as he slapped it into my hand. I bobbed back, not really sure what was happening.

Master Waters turned to the class. "As you know, Mr. Raymond joined us only a few weeks ago. But, under Ms. Andros's tutelage, he advanced quickly. Before class today, I asked Mr. Raymond to go through several of his beginner forms, some one-step fighting moves, and to show me some of the kicks and punches he has learned. He executed them well."

The other fighters clapped, the foam gloves softening the applause. "Because of that, I'm pleased to give him the rank of yellow belt. Congratulations, Mr. Raymond." Another round of applause.

I couldn't help but glance at Jocelyn, who bounced on the balls of her feet and grinned. Max put his gloved hand on her shoulder. Still applauding, Jocelyn moved forward a half-step, making Max's hand drop.

Slipping out my mouth guard, I said, "I owe it all to Jocelyn. Thanks for the extra attention."

"You deserved it!" she shouted back. "I'm so proud of you!"

Lash Boy fumed.

Marshmallow persona aside, I was feeling pretty good going into my first official sparring lesson.

Jocelyn gave me the lowdown on how the class would go. Master Waters would pair fighters, who would have three-minute rounds on large red squares set in the middle of the blue mats that covered the gym's floor. Two fights went on simultaneously, while the rest of the fighters sat on the side, watching and cheering. "Keep an eye on how the other fighters move. Once you know their style, you can use that to your advantage," Jocelyn said.

I let the "keep an eye" comment slide, thanks to the quilt club's insistence that puns are overrated. But I did allow myself a moment to picture truly keeping an eye on other fighters. I was sure I'd have an immediate advantage in the ensuing freak out.

"Why are you laughing?" Jocelyn asked.

"No reason." Snort.

"Awfully cocky for your first time on the mat," said Lash Boy as he sat just to my right.

"Don't try to intimidate him," Jocelyn snapped as she sat down on my left.

"I'm not." Max pulled off his helmet and tucked it under his arm, making his bicep bulge.

"Whatever," Jocelyn and I said at the same time.

All grumbling stopped as Master Waters whistled for attention in the middle of the mat. "All right, fighters. Ready for another Fight Night?"

Around me, kids sitting on the sides of the mat roared. I began to wonder just how much the helmet and gloves actually buffered direct punches and kicks. Like she could read my mind, Jocelyn leaned in and whispered, "The point is to fight with control. Make contact, but don't use full force. You're not going to get knocked out or anything."

"Right," I said. "No worries. Besides, I can take a hit."

This time Max was the one who snorted.

First, Master Waters called on Jocelyn and a black belt named Henry. On the other mat, he called two orange belt kids (one level up from me now). I zeroed in on Henry and Jocelyn's match even though it was much more likely I'd be fighting the other two. Jocelyn was like a blur, kicking and punching, twisting and dodging.

"She's amazing," I said under my breath.

Max pushed air out of his nose in a huff. "She needs to dodge."

I crinkled my eyebrows. "Critical much? She's incredible. She must've kicked him at least five times already."

"Yeah," Max said, "but she *got* kicked at least twice that many. She doesn't duck or block."

I turned back to the fight. As much as I hated to admit this, Max was right. Henry knocked Jocelyn again and again, but it was easy to miss because she didn't even flinch. Just kept flying at him.

"I guess it's because Henry isn't using full force," I said, thinking about what Jocelyn had said to me earlier. "You know, fighting with control."

Max rolled his eyes. "Maybe they started out fighting with control, but they're not anymore."

Sure enough, Henry grunted as his side kick slammed into Jocelyn's waist. Or rather, as Jocelyn slammed into Henry's side kick. She twisted and landed a roundhouse kick, the top of her foot whapping him in the side of the helmet enough to make his head whip to the side. "Use control!" Master Waters barked.

The giant timer on the mat blared at that moment and the three minutes were up. Jocelyn took off her helmet, her face shining with sweat, and her smile glorious. She shook hands with Henry, who took giant gulps of air and rubbed at a spot on his ribs. He didn't smile back, just muttered, "Good fight."

Jocelyn, still grinning, sat cross-legged between me and Max on the side of the mat. "Geez, that felt good," she said.

"What? Getting your butt kicked?" Max grumbled.

"Are you serious? Did you miss the way Henry was limping off the mat?" Jocelyn wiped her forehead with her arm.

"No," Max said. "I also didn't miss the way he landed obvious hits. You would've been out in thirty seconds if that were a tournament."

Jocelyn had explained to me that at tournaments, the objective wasn't to fight for three minutes like here during Fight Night; it was to be the first to land three hits or kicks (five if you were a black belt).

Jocelyn's wide smile wobbled and began to crumble.

"Good thing it's not a tournament," I blurted. "I thought you were incredible."

She bumped against me, her damp hair swinging and knocking me in the neck. "Thanks," she said, then a little louder she added, "I appreciate the support."

Max groaned.

"What?" she snapped.

"You're supposed to be teaching the kid and you can't even acknowledge that defense is just as important as offense. You can't just stand there and be your opponent's punching bag because you can take it standing up. You can't *just* fight. You've got to protect yourself, too!" Max leaned into Jocelyn and hissed all of this, but every kid around could clearly hear him.

Two splotches of red flared on Jocelyn's cheeks. She turned toward Max and hissed right back into his face, "You are not the coach. Do you understand that? You're supposed to be my friend, but you are *not my coach.*"

Max swallowed, the bulge in his throat bopping up and down. Much more quietly, he said, "I thought I was more than just your friend."

Jocelyn squeezed her eyes shut and turned toward the mats again. When she opened her eyes, she looked at the next fight already underway, not at Max. "I thought you were my friend, *too.*"

Max ground his teeth, his jaw clenching with the effort of swallowing down whatever he wanted to say next. What should I have done? Part of me wanted to reach out and grab Jocelyn's trembling hand—whether it was shaking from the adrenaline rush of the fight or this whisper fight I was eavesdropping on, I wasn't sure.

Another part wanted to inch away from them both, knowing this wasn't a fight about her taking too many hits on the mat anymore.

I started to slip off my marshmallow glove, the new Velcro screeching louder the slower I moved. "What are you doing?" Master Waters yelled, just as I slipped it off my hand. "You're up, Mr. Raymond."

"Good luck," Jocelyn said as she turned to me. "Remember, be first if you can."

"And dodge," Max snapped.

I sucked in a mouthful of air before slipping in my mouth guard. I pushed the helmet onto my head, ignoring the way it made my headache pound even harder, and lowered the plastic shield over my face. I strapped on the glove again as I trotted out to the mat where the beginners were fighting. "All right, fighters," Master Waters said. "As you know, this is Mr. Raymond's first Fight Night." Another round of roars from the group. "Good luck, Mr. Raymond. We don't take it easy on newbies here at Waters Martial Arts. We're kicking off your fighting career by going toe-to-toe with our very own pint-sized killer."

Up popped Peggy. (Remember her? The pigtailed kid barking at me to "Dig! Dig! Dig!" on my very first practice?) She ripped out the pigtail elastics and slammed a bubblegum-pink helmet on. When she stepped onto the mat—and I'm not making this up—she growled. A deep, guttural, I'm-about-to-kick-butt-and-take-names growl. I stepped backward. Master Waters pushed me forward. I'm pretty sure he laughed while doing so.

"Haha," I said. "Very funny. Who am I really going to fight?" Peggy stood across from me, her head barely reaching my armpits. Upper belt or not, the kid would fly across the mat the first time I kicked her.

This time I knew Master Waters laughed. In fact, everyone did. Everyone but Jocelyn, who shouted out, "Use your legs! Don't let her get past your kick or you're in trouble!"

Seriously? I was going to fight a ten-year-old little girl? Peggy growled again as the timer dinged. She stormed toward me, a blur of side kicks. *Kick, kick, kick, kick, kick!* I backed away from her. Picture the whirl of a hummingbird's wings, so fast you can barely register the movement. That was Peggy. *Kickkickkickkickkick!*

I panicked, back-stepping on the red square of the mat with Peggy in hot pursuit like a demonic doll. *Bam, bam, bam!* She nailed me in the ribs. I noticed her toenails were painted and sparkly for just a second before freaking out because she was totally after me again! I stepped onto the blue and Master Waters pushed me back in. "Fight, kid," he ordered. "Fight!"

I twisted so my good eye faced Peggy's whirling kicks of death. The shield steamed up from my panic sweats. Waiting until she was just about to slam me with her teeny tiny sparkly foot, I sidestepped, remembering Jocelyn's endless drills with the handheld target—where she'd whip the target toward me in different directions and I'd sidestep and hit. Sidestep and hit. Sidestep-and-hit.

So I did. At the last second I sidestepped and made contact with my fist to the side of Peggy's helmet. It knocked her helmet sideways a little. For the first time since the fight began, she lowered her foot. She readjusted her helmet. Her brown eyes narrowed, and she growled again.

And then I got my butt kicked by a ten-year-old in front of my dream girl and her boyfriend.

"*Cah, cah, cah!*"

Oh, joy. Gramps had showed up in time for the fight, too.

Master Waters pulled me aside after class. "You did well today, Mr. Raymond."

I almost shoved off the hand he slapped down on my shoulder and said, "Yeah, right." But then I remembered I was talking with Master Waters. "It didn't feel like I did a good job, sir."

Master Waters grinned. "Peggy's been training since she was three. She's a machine. Her biggest weapon is cuteness. No one expects her to be as fierce as she is."

I nodded.

"There's a lesson there, son," Master Waters went on.

"Grow some pigtails?"

He looked remarkably like Max when he was annoyed. Teeth clenching and everything. "No," Master Waters said. "What I mean is, Peggy knows she's adorable. Instead of fighting it, she uses it. Take what could be a disadvantage and turn it on people you're up against."

"So you're telling me to eyeball what sets me apart and exploit the heck out of it."

"Exactly," Master Waters said, not even blinking at the eyeball comment. Like I said, the worst thing in the world is having to explain a joke, so I just let it go.

Funny thing, after sparring, I noticed that my headache was completely gone.

Chapter Sixteen

Over the next few classes, Master Waters pulled me from going over forms and punches with the rest of the beginners to spar with different students.

"You pick up the forms much faster than the others," he said by way of explanation. I didn't mention that it's because I have zero social life, so I pretty much go over my forms all night. But sparring is something you actually have to practice with another person.

The extra attention helped a lot. By our next Fight Night, I held my own against Peggy the Pigtailed Bringer of Pain. A month of intense classes later, I was sparring new opponents, even a few green belts.

I thought about what Master Waters said. Soon I saw my advantage (*saw*—haha! I just can't help myself.). No one I fought wanted to make—or keep—eye contact. Therefore, I stared them down. And since we were so close while fighting, I could see where their eyes moved. Every single one of them let their eyes dart to wherever they were about to attack. Sometimes their eyes flicked

to my head, cluing me in to block there. Other times their gaze was at my ribs, shoulder, or stomach. I became an absolute master of blocking. Sidestep-and-hit.

"That was awesome!" Jocelyn cheered for me a few months later when I fought Henry and didn't die. The guy's a black belt. Just landing a few hits here and there was amazing. Every punch Henry landed was on my right side and happened when I was on the offensive. Not bad, you know?

"Well, I had a pretty incredible coach," I said. Okay, picture me here. Yeah, fights are only three minutes, but you're talking about nonstop dodging, punching, kicking, whirling, ducking, and jumping for all one hundred and eighty seconds. Coming off the mat felt a lot like stepping out of a swimming pool. I was drenched, my legs and arms felt weighed down. I yanked off the helmet and face shield and fist bumped Jocelyn. (Honesty alert: part of me thought I probably looked pretty amazing—my bright red hair darkened with sweat, muscles tense and outlined on my arms, chiseled features shining. All these workouts were giving me actual muscles, broadening my shoulders, and making me look pretty tough, I thought. The gym was lined with mirrors that I was careful not to look at so as not to shatter the illusion and find out I looked more like when the General gets stuck in the rain.) I gave Jocelyn a rakish smile.

"It's the blocking that sets you apart," Max cut in.

Jocelyn's face set and I knew she was about to go off on Lash Boy. It's strange: at school, they were always perfectly in sync. Always together. Always smiling. Always choking-on-cotton-candy sickly sweet. But on Fight Night—or at least the Fight Nights I'd been to—they were ready to rip each other apart like a pair of lions.

Even weirder: Max and I were sort of becoming friends. I mean, it's a tough thing to hate the person who went out of his way to make sure you got to the right class on time, thanks to that bright green electric tape. Then there were the Wednesday night classes, when Jocelyn taught the beginners and Max worked through sparring with me on another mat, under Master Waters's orders. At first, he just went through the motions. But here's the thing: Max Waters is such an incredibly, annoyingly good guy, he couldn't help but high-five me when I landed my first tornado kick (yes, it's as killer as it sounds). When we sparred each other, at first he just grunted out commands ("My ribs are open! Where's your punch?") and basically let me land punches and kicks on him. Soon, I was getting better, and he was actually huffing and puffing, dodging and ducking, as we fought. I saw we were pretty alike, both of us focusing entirely on the fight. Both of us full in.

One Wednesday as we waited for class to start at the gym, I saw him make a mistake on his math homework. We were sitting on the plastic chairs by the entrance, killing time. Max basically lived at the gym, so it wasn't unusual for him to be doing his homework in between taking and teaching classes. I almost ignored the mistake he made, my gaze shifting to where Jocelyn was warming up on the mat. But then I remembered that electric green tape. I took a deep breath inside. "Take another look at number six. Remember, you're solving for the slope of the line caused by the equation. Not for x or y."

"What does that even mean?" Max rubbed at his eyes. "If I fail another quiz, Dad's head will explode. Does your dad freak out over grades?"

I swallowed. "My dad's not around," I said.

"Oh. Sorry." Max's face flushed.

"I talked to him about a week and a half ago, but he never asks about grades or anything. I don't think he even knows what I'm studying."

"Sorry, man," Max said. "I didn't realize your folks aren't together."

"No, I mean he and Mom aren't divorced or anything. They're, like, sickeningly in love. He's just doing an assignment in Alaska." For a second, I thought about the club's quiltervention and almost spilled about Dad's work, about going on assignment with him in the past, about missing him. "Never mind, it's complicated."

Max's mouth popped open, but before he could ask a question or, worse, give another apology, I pointed to the problem. Maybe it's the scientists-for-parents genes, but my math skills are tight. "Try getting just x and y on one side." And that's how I started sort of tutoring Max in math before karate classes.

Soon, he and I were fist bumping when we passed each other in the hall. Soon, I had a seat kicked out for me at his table in the cafeteria (never beside Jocelyn, of course). Soon, we were sort of friends, which made the whole nonstop crushing on his girlfriend extra awkward.

Before I knew it, Christmas was over (picture a Rudolphesque yard horse). Then Easter (Yep. Bunny-eared yard horse). Suddenly it was April (yard horse with flowery umbrella), and I wore a green belt, having passed my orange belt test, too.

Pushing aside all these errant thoughts and partly to distract Jocelyn from launching into a fight with my sort-of-friend Max (you didn't forget where I was, did you? I just got off the mat after fighting Henry, the black belt), I said, "I wish I could lose the face shield." I wiped at the steamed-up plastic with my uniform T-shirt. About a minute and a half in, it really fogged up, making it tough to keep eye contact.

"Yeah, well, you're going to have to deal with it, right?" Jocelyn said.

"Looking good out there, Richie Ryder!" Gramps called from the back of the room. He made it a point to be there for every Fight Night—ever since the first time I got my butt kicked. I thought at first it was just because he loved seeing Peggy beat the stuffing out of me, but now he actually cheered for me—something that drove Master Waters nuts.

Master Waters glared at Gramps for calling out during class but without as much heat as usual. "Very nice, son," Master Waters said to me. "Has Jocelyn or Max told you about the upcoming tournament?"

"Do you think he's ready for that?" Jocelyn and Max said at the same time. Same words, same time, very different sentences. Coming from Jocelyn, it sounded excited. Like, "Can you believe it? You're going to win a trophy at a tournament!" From Max, it sounded like a death sentence. Like, "Can you believe it? You're going to die at a tournament."

Master Waters pointed to Max and then out at the mat. "You're up, son," he said, then called out another black belt's name to go fight Max. Turning back to me, he said, "It's in a week, Mr. Raymond. You'll be facing dozens of martial artists from all over Virginia. We always bring home the hardware from tournaments." He motioned to the trophies lining the gym as he walked backward toward the sparring matches. "Train hard."

Jocelyn squealed and wrapped her arms around me in a hug. "That's so awesome!" I stiffened, suddenly remembering how entirely sweaty and stinky I was. Jocelyn froze, suddenly remembering—I'm guessing—her boyfriend was just a few feet away. But even worse was when she pulled back. A second or two of electricity, invisible but everywhere, shot between us when our faces were only inches apart. It prickled up and down my arMs. For a stupid second my face tilted even more toward hers. For a second I thought I was going to kiss her.

"Jocelyn!" Master Waters barked from back on the mat. "Get ready to fight!"

We both whipped around, just in time to see Max take a straight shot to the face, his eyes on us instead of his opponent.

Luckily the next day was Saturday, so I wouldn't have to face Jocelyn or Max at school.

"Besides, *nothing* actually happened," I told Alice as we FaceTimed. I was lying on my bed, staring up at the ceiling and pretty much hating myself. Alice nodded, her white-blonde hair swinging forward.

"Sure," she said. "Nothing happened. We just spent twenty minutes dissecting each and every second of nothing."

I sighed. "Fine. Something happened. But nothing *really* happened."

"Sure."

"Alice!"

"Ryder!"

There was a quick *rap, rap, rap* on my door. "Are you talking to a girl in there?" Gramps bellowed behind it.

"I'll be out in a minute!" I yelled.

"Try to kiss on one girl one day, spend all morning talking to another the next," Gramps grumped just loud enough for Alice to hear. Yeah, Gramps had been watching *everything* at Fight Night.

Alice laughed. "Looks like even Gramps saw *nothing* happen."

"Look," I snapped, "I didn't actually kiss her. I didn't do anything wrong, okay? So, we hugged. Friends hug all the time. I hugged you, like, every other hour when we were at Addison."

"You *are* a hugger," Alice admitted.

"Yeah, and Lucas never freaked out about it," I pointed out.

"Well, he never actually saw it." Alice's lips quivered the way they always do when she knows she said something funny and is waiting to hear if you'll go with it or not.

"That's just wrong," I said, but not able to keep from laughing. Lucas was born without eyes, so of course he never saw us hugging.

When the quiet after our laughter stretched too long, I asked, "How is Lucas, anyway? I never hear from him."

Alice shifted a little. "We broke up, actually."

"Oh."

Alice shrugged. "We're talking about you, remember?"

"But what happened?" I asked.

She shook her head. "We're fine. Just didn't work out. Lucas and I are younger than you. I mean, we're thirteen. I'm pretty sure relationships are supposed to last a couple weeks at our age, tops. In fact, my brother rolls his eyes every time I even utter the word relationship."

"Yeah," I snorted. "Not like the mature, long-lasting relationships inherent in one-eyed, ginger fourteen-year-olds."

"Shut up." Alice sighed. "Quit doing that."

"Doing what?"

"Making yourself a joke."

"Have you been talking to my quilting club?"

In the weeks following my quiltervention, Janet May, Madelyn, Jess, and Miss Singer had given up on getting me to dish on my inner feelings and had gone back to just handing me needles to thread. But Janet May shook her head at me a lot. And Miss Singer gave me a blank notebook like the one she carried around all the time—just in case I felt like writing stuff down. I actually had skipped the last few classes.

Alice ignored me. "I don't know, Ryder."

"What don't you know?" I asked.

"I think you started off liking Jocelyn, but you really started liking her when you saw she was with Max. You had, like, a problem with him from the moment you met him."

I shook my head. "He did immediately call me a freak."

Alice tilted her head in agreement. "Right, but don't you think part of why you like Jocelyn is because it bothers Max?"

"I've got to go," I said abruptly. And it wasn't just because I didn't want to admit that maybe Alice was right. I really did have to leave. Gramps was dragging me to a fundraiser for Logan's community project—the center he wanted to create for people in mourning.

"No, don't go like that," Alice said, pulling the phone in closer. Her eyes fluttered like lightning bugs. "I'm not trying to upset you. I just think you've got to figure out what your problem with Max is and how much of *that* is why you're so into Jocelyn."

"You're reading way too much into this. What could I possibly have against Max? He's the freaking home-town hero. The most decent, all-around greatest guy who ever went to Papuaville Middle School. Everybody loves Max Waters."

"Sounds a lot like how Ryder Raymond was at Addison." Alice cocked an eyebrow. "Yeah, what could possibly be your problem?"

Rap, rap, rap. Gramps drummed on the door again. "Come on, Richie Ryder! We've got to get going."

"Sorry, Alice," I said. "I really do have to go. Gramps wants me to go with him to a fundraiser for a Grief Center this guy Logan is trying to start." I realized my voice was way too chipper for the topic.

"Ryder!" she called, but I pretended not to hear as I pressed the end button.

Chapter Seventeen

aybe calling the event a fundraiser was a bit of a stretch.

Really, it was just a hot dog and lemonade stand outside of the Home Depot being run by a bunch of Boy Scouts with handmade posters. The quilting club was represented, too, with Janet May and Madelyn selling squares with the Papuaville Guinea Pigs stitched onto them for five bucks a pop. Janet May's guinea pigs had their tiny paws clasped in prayer on her squares.

"Hey," I said to the girls.

Madelyn rolled her eyes at me. Janet May crossed her arMs. "We've missed you the last few quilting clubs, Richie Ryder."

"I've been checking out other experientials," I said.

"Or avoiding us."

I busied myself checking out the squares. Madelyn's was easy to pick out. It was just a guinea pig skull with flower eye sockets. I chuckled and almost said something about it being a bit dark for a grief center fundraiser—or

maybe about her personal style really beginning to blos-som—but I bit it back. Janet May buried the square under the others when I dropped it, and Madelyn looked away.

The squares were displayed next to Logan's laptop, which ran a loop of a PowerPoint display featuring quotes from the people he interviewed, followed by a plea for contributions.

I missed most of the quotes since I had to stand awkwardly close to the screen to read them. A little voice in my head whispered that I had to get a lot closer than I should've—than I used to—but I told that voice to shut its fool mouth. When I made out a pic-ture of Gramps next to the yard horse, I leaned in to read his quote. *"Well, I keep her memory alive. I dress up the (yard) horse, you see . . ." HELP AREA WIDOWS AND WIDOWERS FIND SAFE,* HEALTHY *OUTLETS FOR THEIR GRIEF.*

"Taken a bit out of context," Gramps said around a mouthful of hot dog.

I shrugged, remembering how the yard horse cur-rently was decked out with a flowery umbrella and a basket filled with gardening tools. "How soon until you can get this center off the ground, Logan?" I asked.

Ever since the whole caught-in-my-underwear moment, Logan has had trouble directly addressing me. He sort of gazed over my head and said, "I'm not sure

I'll be able to open an actual center, as in it being its own building. But I'm hoping we can start having group meetings by the end of the year."

"That's awesome!" came an incredibly earnest voice to my right.

I swiveled my head to confirm what I already knew. Yep, the one person I had been hoping to avoid for the rest of my life—or at very least the weekend—was standing there. Lash Boy himself. He loosely held hands with the person I simultaneously couldn't wait to see and also wanted to avoid forever.

"Hey, Jocelyn," I muttered, realizing too late I probably should've said hi to Max first. You know, because *nothing happened with Jocelyn the day before.*

"Hey," she said softly, her cheeks flushing.

Bam! Electricity shot from nowhere in this crystal-blue-sky day, sizzling between us as we stared too long at each other. Man, her eyes were a liquid caramel brown. Her mouth, apple red.

I shook my head and stepped back. Too late, I held out a fist for Max to bump. His eyes flicked between us. He bumped my fist and turned back to Logan. I turned, too, deliberately putting Jocelyn on my blind side.

Unfortunately, that also put me face to face with Janet May. "Richie Ryder, what are you doing?" Her voice dripped with disappointment.

"Whatever, Janet May," I hissed. "You don't know anything about me, remember?"

She shook her head. "When you're not making stupid jokes you can be really mean. Or maybe just stupid." She sighed. "We really do miss you at quilting club, though."

"I miss you, too, Janet May."

Gramps and I were each downing our second hot dogs when the fight began. At first, it wasn't too obvious. Just a conversation that slowly got louder and louder at the outskirts of the small crowd around Logan's stand. It was to my right, so I wasn't really paying attention to it. But when I heard, "Max, I don't want to talk about this!" all but screamed by Jocelyn, I turned around.

Max and Jocelyn faced off, Logan in between them, a few feet from where we gathered. All around us, voices snuffed out. Janet May glared at me like whatever they were fighting about had to do with me. I put up my hands like, "Hey, I'm all the way over here!"

Still, against better judgment, I edged a little closer.

"I'm just saying it's a great idea!" Max said, his voice quieter now. "Think of all the people we could help!"

"Will you stop already?" Jocelyn hissed. "I'm so sick of your nonstop gotta-help-everyone-all-the-time crap!"

"Crap?" Max reared back like she had slapped him. "You and me, we've got so much to be grateful for. We—I mean, *I* need to pay it forward, okay?"

"Enough already! Just shut up, Max!" Jocelyn's face was scary red. She pulled on her sleeves with her fingertips and crossed her arMs. She was too far away for me to see, but based on how her voice shook I was pretty sure she either was crying or was about to start.

Logan stepped backward, unwittingly opening up the little circle to include me, since I was lurking just behind them. "I-I really don't want to get involved with this," he said.

Max threw out an arm to him. "Just tell her, Logan. Tell her how easy it was to get this project started."

Logan cleared his throat. "It wasn't too much work, I guess."

"And what did you just say seemed to help people the most?" Max prompted.

Reluctantly, like the words were soaked in lemon juice, Logan uttered, "Talking about their pain. The therapists and the grieving people I spoke with said talking about the experiences helped them deal with them the most."

Logan turned slightly and glanced at Gramps. When he saw the old man was zeroed in on our conversation, he quickly looked away. "Once they talk about it, they can move on. Until then, they're sort of stuck there."

"Yeah, but what if they like where they are?" Gramps muttered.

"Think about it," Max said, his voice pleading. He stepped a little closer to Jocelyn, who sidestepped. Again making me part of the circle. "We could, I don't know, go into elementary schools. Talk about fire safety. With our history, we could really impact the community. Make a difference." He bit his lip, then went on. "Think about it, taking what happened to Jacob and—"

"No!" Jocelyn yelped. She put her hands over her ears like a little child.

"Come on, Jocelyn. It's been *years*. He'd want us to keep other kids from going through what we—"

"*Shut up!*"

Without thinking, I put my hand on Jocelyn's shoulder. "Listen, maybe you guys should talk about this another time," I said quietly.

Max rounded on me. "She's never going to talk about it. Ever."

I felt a shudder roll through Jocelyn. "I'm so sorry to deprive you of another freaking cause, Max!" she roared.

Max's face whitened. "What are you talking about?"

Around us, people stopped in their tracks and stared. A little quieter but just as shaky, Jocelyn said, "When are you going to stop trying to save people? When? You're never going to make up for it! He's still going to be dead!"

216

Max shook his head, his face as white as Alice's. "That's not—I'm not trying—"

I felt my fingers squeeze Jocelyn's birdlike shoulder. Max reached out for her, too, but Jocelyn stepped away, so that her back was inches from my chest.

"I know he's gone," Max whispered. "I just think if any good could come from it . . ." he took a deep breath, ". . . then it might make sense . . ."

Jocelyn shook her head. "Shut up," she whispered, her eyes clenched shut.

"Jocelyn, you're going to have to deal with it someday. Why not like this?"

"No," I found myself saying. All right, shouting. But those words: *going to have to deal with it.* They rattled around my head. "No, she doesn't have to." I stepped around Jocelyn so I was just in front of her. "If she doesn't want to talk about it, she doesn't have to."

Max's hands curled into fists. "You don't know what you're talking about."

And you know what? I didn't. I didn't have any idea what Jocelyn was dealing with. I never met her brother. I certainly hadn't been there right before he died, as Max had been. I didn't know what it was like to lose a friend. Lose a brother. But I did know what it was like to have person after person question the way you deal with things. Pushing you to feel things—feel pain, anger, grief—when the truth is, it was just as easy, *even easier*, to push those feelings away. Yeah, you had to forget about what life was like before. But sometimes that made today a whole heck of a lot easier.

"Just, just," Max said, standing on his toes to look over me at Jocelyn. His voice was thick with passion and pain and so much earnestness. "Just *let yourself remember*. Do you remember, Jocelyn? What it was like *before*?"

"Stop," Jocelyn whispered. Standing there, with Jocelyn vibrating with pain just behind me, everything I pushed aside started to boil in me, too. I couldn't let that happen. Not to either of us.

I punched Max Waters in the face.

The wet, brittle sound of Max Waters's nose squashing under my fist echoed in my head for hours.

"You saw it," I said to Gramps on the way home. "His hands were fisted. He was going to punch me. I just did it first."

Gramps didn't speak. Didn't look at me, either.

We got home and Gramps stomped inside. He let the screen door slam shut before I was able to come in. I'm not sure if that meant I wasn't allowed in or if it was just him being angry. Either way, I couldn't enter. Not into the dark little house where the squelching sound of Max's nose would bounce around even louder.

I sat down next to the yard horse and worked on breathing in and out. Any second now, Max Waters was going to show up and pummel me into pieces. Or worse, Max Waters and his dad would come here and pummel me to pieces. Or worst yet, Master Waters was going to kick me out of Waters Martial Arts. I knew the policy—anyone who fought outside of self-defense was immediately up for expulsion. (And my mind snagged a bit on the idea that he could *literally* kick me out of the studio.)

I closed my eyes and lay flat on the grass. Another failed coping attempt of Mom and Dad's after getting Artie was meditation. One thing I remember was the instructor—this gray-haired woman who smelled like oranges and seemed more like a grandma than a spiritual adviser—told me to lie on my back and picture my spine fusing with the planet. Try to feel the Earth rotate with me going along for the ride. It was supposed to center me or something.

I tried that now, lying there on my back, eyes closed, and breathing in and out. I almost did it—almost blissed out for a moment and lost the squelching echo. Then something landed with a thud on my chest and I knew my time on Earth was over. Max Waters was about to stomp me to death.

I opened my eyes (fine, eye) and saw not Max Waters's foot but the General, curled up on my stomach. Maybe she was trying to suffocate me. Since death was imminent, I risked petting her. The General began to purr, as though she too could sense I wasn't long for this world.

My cellphone buzzed in my back pocket. Huh. It seemed a hastily written goodbye-forever text (*Hey Dad, I punched a black belt kid and broke his nose. This is probably the last you'll hear from me. Thanks for being an okay dad. Over and out.*) was what it took to finally get the man to pick up his phone.

I let the call go to voicemail and closed my eyes.

Sure enough, a minute later I felt another buzz. That would be Mom.

A minute after that, Gramps's home phone rang. Distantly, I heard him huff, "Your dang son's gone batty, that's what's going on. Punched a kid for no good reason." Careful not to disturb the General, I fished out my phone. I plugged in my headphones and turned on my sad music soundtrack. I didn't realize I was singing along until Jocelyn yanked out one earbud and said, "That's your plan? Find a river to skate away on?" She stepped forward so her shadow went over me.

I shrugged to cover up embarrassment at singing Joni Mitchell. I almost blurted that when I was just a little kid Mom used to play the folk singer's music over and over while I napped on the couch during my treatments. But I didn't. The General lazily hissed at my body's movement. "Seems as good a plan as any."

Jocelyn lowered herself on the grass next to me, plugging the earbud into her own ear. For a few minutes we just listened to the sad music.

"How dead am I?" I asked, looking up at the cloudless sky.

Gramps had grabbed me after the punch, pulling me to the car, but I had seen Jocelyn take a Guinea Pig quilt patch and hold it under Max's bleeding nose as we pulled away.

She pulled in a big breath. "The doctor reset his nose. Max told his dad some story about you turning suddenly and knocking him. The doc said it's going to take about six weeks to heal entirely. So no tournament for Max."

"Wait!" I said. "He lied to his dad?"

"Yeah."

"Did Master Waters buy it?" I asked.

Jocelyn nodded.

"Why would he do that for me? I mean, if he told the truth, I'd be in huge trouble. And I'd definitely be off the team." I didn't mention the ongoing waking nightmare I'd been having about being arrested for assault. That could happen, too.

"That's who Max is. He always takes the high road. Always does the right thing." She cleared her throat. "He broke up with me."

Neither of us spoke for a long time, letting song after song pull at our thoughts. "Why did you do it?" she whispered.

"I don't know."

Jocelyn stretched out her arms so that the tops of our hands brushed. I braced myself for another round of electricity to zap between us. But it only felt like her hand touching mine.

Chapter Eighteen

Mom sat at the kitchen table across from me, staring me down. She had her cellphone, featuring Dad's scary face via FaceTime, propped up on a stack of books. "What is going on?" she demanded.

"Nothing." I stared at my hands.

"Something is going on, otherwise you wouldn't have broken that kid's nose!"

I shrugged.

"Ryder!" Mom and Dad both yelled in unison.

I sat back in the chair and crossed my arMs. "It was a mistake, all right? I didn't mean to punch him."

"How do you accidentally punch someone in the face?" Dad asked.

I glared at his face on the screen. "I don't know, Dad. How do you accidentally forget to call someone back for six days in a row?"

Dad's face moved off screen for a second and I heard him huff like one of his bison. "This isn't about me, son. You know how tough it is to get reception out here. I

223

had to abandon my research and drive fifty miles this afternoon so I could have this conversation."

"Thanks for your sacrifice," I muttered.

Mom's eyes widened. "What has gotten into you, Ryder? You know we're here for you when you need us. Don't blame this on your father, not when I'm in the same house as you. Why haven't you come to me to discuss this problem?"

I shook my head. "Forget it. It's not your fault."

Dad cleared his throat. "Then what is going on? Gramps said all this is about some girl?"

Was it? Was it all about Jocelyn? Maybe a little. But mostly I just had to, in that moment, shut up Max.

"It's this guy. He's so freaking perfect all the time. I just got sick of it."

Mom stared at me. Dad stared at me. Dad cleared his throat. "Let me get this straight. You punched the kid—breaking his nose—because he was too nice of a guy?"

I shrugged again.

"I'm not buying it," Dad said. "We raised you better than that."

I coughed but it sounded a lot like a snort.

"What's that supposed to mean?" asked Mom, her voice high.

"Nothing." I stared at my hands.

"Whatever your reason was, we need to deal with it now," Mom said. Again those words rattled in my thick skull. *Deal with it.* She pushed a notebook and a pencil toward me. "I want you to write this boy a letter. An apology."

I picked up the pencil and twirled it in my fingers. "There's no point," I finally said.

"Why would you say that, Ryder?" asked Mom, her hand stretching out to squeeze mine.

I held up the pencil. There seriously was no point on it. (That one was for you, quilt club!) I threw down the pencil, bolted up from the chair, and went to my room, slamming the door.

It was late evening when Mom opened my bedroom door without knocking. "Grab your jacket," she said. "We're leaving."

"Where are we going?" I asked, thinking she was going to ruin everything—including (okay, especially) Max's lie to his dad that this was all an accident—and force me to apologize in person.

"There's a massive mayfly bug swarm in Pennsylvania. We're going on a road trip."

Seriously, this is my mom's idea of family bonding, chasing bugs.

But they weren't just any bugs.

Mom put the station wagon into park next to a bridge in a small Pennsylvania town, putting an end to the most suffocating, quiet road trip in the history of bad road trips. (Seriously, Mom didn't turn on the radio once in two hours and thirteen minutes.)

I wondered how we had managed to travel into a different temperate zone.

Because it was snowing in Wrightsville, Pennsylvania.

In the middle of May.

Thick flakes shone in the yellow glow of streetlights and the full moon, a total whiteout on the roadway.

"What?" I stammered.

Mom smiled. "Can you believe it?" In front of us was a bridge with police cars blocking both sides. Officers stood near the bridge, shaking their heads. "They've actually closed traffic, the little pests."

"Those are . . . those are bugs?"

"Mayflies," Mom said happily. Thousands—no, *millions*—of tiny flying bugs clouded the sky. It was as thick as any blizzard I had seen in Montana one winter.

Mom handed me a surgical mask. "You're going to want to put up your hood, too. They love to fly into ears. And don't take off your glasses."

"Are we seriously going out in this?"

"Watch your step," she said instead of answering. "It's going to be slippery." She put her hand on the door handle. "And take a deep breath."

I half expected a blast of cold air to hit me in the face when the door opened. What actually happened was much, much worse. The shudder-inducing aroma of roadkill mixed with pond scum and a dash of decaying fish slammed me in the face. "OMG!" I gasped.

"I know!" Mom chirped, and she twirled. She actually *twirled* in a flurry of bugs.

We approached the officers so Mom could flash her credentials. "Dr. Jenna Raymond," Mom said with a flourish, like she was a secret agent or something, "Entomologist." Each step made a crunching sound under our heels, a lot like a much drier version of breaking Max's nose, as we stepped on the bodies of fallen bugs. Getting out a small ruler from her bag, Mom hooted. "Two inches thick! Can you believe this?"

No, I could not.

"Oh, Ryder," she gushed, nothing but round eyes behind her glasses. "I was so worried we'd miss this."

Mom got out a camera and took dozens of pictures, mostly for work but a few of me, too. She pulled out a few specimen tubes and added mayflies to them.

One of the officers ambled over to us. "You're certainly the only person we've seen who's happy about this invasion. Three motorcycles went down trying to cross the bridge last night. A minivan nearly went over the railing."

"Sorry to hear that," Mom said, "but this invasion is actually good news for your community."

The officer and I looked around at the buzzing blizzard. His mouth popped open, but just for a second (too many bugs to keep it gaping for long).

I couldn't see Mom's smile under her mask, but I heard it in her voice. "A population this size could only emerge if the river below us is significantly cleared of pollutants. In other words, this is proof your town's pollution controls are working! Mayflies are a vital indicator of our water systems' health. Congratulations!"

The officer stared at Mom for a full thirty seconds. He absently slapped at a mayfly on his nose. Another one immediately took its place. Turning to me, he said, "Is she for real?"

I nodded.

"No need to get testy," Mom said. "Two days max and they'll all be dead."

"Thank goodness." The officer crunched away, stepping a bit harder than necessary.

Mom sighed. "He just doesn't get it."

"Got to say, Mom, I don't get it, either."

Mom pulled me under a street lamp, so the yellow glow illuminated the swarm. "Try to focus on just one bug, Ryder." It was tough with how quickly they moved, but finally I found one. It bobbed up and down, up and down, then suddenly back and forth. Quickly it went up and down again.

Mom, her eyes on me instead of the bug, said, "It's a nuptial dance. The dancers are all male. Females fly through the swarm and join with a mate. A little later, the female lays eggs over the river. Up to three thousand of them!"

"What then?" I asked, giving a little admiring nod when I saw that one little guy found a special friend midair.

"She's spent, drifts to the top of the river, and dies over her eggs. By then, the male also has fallen. In fact, I'd say just about all of these under our feet are danced-out males. They try to follow their mate to the river, to make sure she deposits the eggs safely, but they're usually too exhausted to make it the whole way."

Mom held out her hand. One of the bugs landed on her fingertip. "They're so tiny, aren't they? But fascinating. Those eggs might spend up to a year in the river, turning into elongated nymphs. They find their way to the side of the river and sprout tiny wings. Within hours, they transform again, into this." I'm not positive if it was *my* bug, but as she spoke I watched another dancer fall to the ground.

She held the bug out under my nose. "See how beautiful he is?"

"Sorry, Mom," I said. "I mean, I get it, they're cool and all. But beautiful is a stretch."

Mom let the bug drift from her fingertip. "Under a microscope, you can see these are bright, beautiful insects. Their delicate wings remind me of stained-glass windows, and then there are their long narrow bodies. Their entire adult life consists of only a few hours. They never eat, never rest. Just ensure the next generation will be created. A generation they'll never know."

Mom turned to me. "Humans, we're not like that. Our lives grow more and more complicated after our children are born. We have decades ahead of us. But if this was what life was like for us—one beautiful dance before dying—in order to make sure you would be born, I'd be first in line to buy my party ticket."

I didn't know what to say. Silently, we made our way back to the car, laughing as we slipped a little on the sheet of bugs.

Mom packed up her samples before taking her place next to me in the car. She turned on the engine, but left the car in park. We watched the pulsating dance of death and birth illuminated by the station wagon's headlights for a few more moments. For just a second, I got it. I understood what fascinated her so much about insects.

When she put the car in reverse and we left the bridge behind us, I asked, "Mom, why did you take me here?"

She didn't answer for a long time. Finally, she pulled off the highway and onto an access road. I couldn't make out her features in the darkness. It was so long before she spoke that clouds drifted away from the moon and suddenly there she was, her pale face blue in the moonlight, eyes watery and wide.

"Do you remember when you were small? Before?" She took a deep breath. "Before you had cancer?"

I shook my head, wanting to turn away from her but not able to.

"There was a swarm the night before the doctor's appointment when you were diagnosed. Not of mayflies, but of lightning bugs. The thing is, your dad and I, we're scientists. We knew as soon as we saw the white glow of your pupils in photographs that something was wrong. We're expert researchers. We knew what the doctor was going to tell us the next morning. But you didn't." She sighed. "So we went to the swarm. Are you sure you don't remember this?"

I shook my head. "I don't have a lot of memories from before," I said quietly.

Mom swallowed and nodded. Her smile was slow and soft. "You danced with the bugs as they flashed around you. It looked—it looked like the stars came down from the sky just so you could play among them. You never noticed your father crying in the car."

"Dad cried?" I couldn't picture my bulking giant of a father weeping.

"He curled up like one of the spent mayflies, sobbing." Mom shifted. "I stood with you, watching you play, thinking about the unfairness of it all. All your life, we took you with us on our research trips. You knew more about insects than you did the alphabet. You could set up a tent in less time than it took most kids your age to snap a few LEGO bricks together into a tower. We thought we were giving you a magical life, but really it was just an extension of *our* life." Mom let her fingers run down the side of my cheek. "But there we were, surrounded by death and birth, and I realized—maybe for the first time—that you weren't an extension of your father and me. You were you. You had your own life. And if that life was going to end prematurely, there wasn't anything—*anything*—I could do about it."

"Mom . . ."

"Ryder, none of this is coming out right. You know I never knew my parents, right? They died when I was small."

I nodded.

"I only ever knew *me*. I was scared, knowing what you were about to face, that you only knew us. That you might never have a chance to know *you*."

"I don't understand," I muttered.

"Then there was your father," Mom went on as if I hadn't spoken, "raised by Gramps, whose life was and still is entirely tied up with his dead wife. When we thought we might lose you, too, your dad panicked, knowing he'd never get over it, the way his dad never got over losing his mom."

"Okay . . ."

"We promised ourselves something in the car that day. We swore that we'd get you through this. That we'd fight like crazy for you—and push you to fight just as much. That we'd make sure you always had what you needed." Mom bit her lip and stared at me intently for a second. "And we swore—we promised—that no matter what happened, we wouldn't lose each other or ourselves in the ever-changing, buzzing cycle of life we found ourselves in."

My head pounded—maybe it was the effect of the mayflies—but I couldn't seem to understand what she was saying.

"We went too far, though, didn't we?" she said. "We respected your independence too much. So much that we made you feel alone. We're scientists," she said again, "yet we somehow didn't question the evidence in front of us: you. Choosing to believe that if you were laughing or making us laugh, you weren't hurting. That if you never spoke about life before your diagnosis, you never thought about it. That you got a second shot—a second pair of wings—and we shouldn't question it."

Mom took a shaky breath. "And there's more."

I cocked an eyebrow at her, making her laugh. But it was nervous sounding and I noticed her lips trembling a bit.

"We were scared," she said quietly. "We came so close to losing you. We had to think about what life would be like if we didn't have you. We decided that if we got you through treatment, we would continue building our careers, our lives, separate from our lives as parents and spouses. We told ourselves it was to show you through our unconventional lives the importance of independence. Of following your passion. But it's really because we were scared." Quieter, she added, "It's stupid, though. Because I'm still scared. All the time."

I looked away, thinking of erasing the doctor appointment message. "Scared of what?"

Mom surprised me by not mentioning the *c* word at all. "Scared that I'm doing a bad job as a parent. What you saw today—it's proof that nature shows us again and again and again that our most important job while on this Earth, the most vital purpose, is making sure the next generation thrives. I'm terrified to mess that up."

Mom smiled at me, sort of wobbly. "I think I'm doing an okay job. That I've got a kind, funny, charismatic boy. But then he goes and breaks another boy's nose."

"Mom . . ."

"I know, I know," she said. "I am just so scared that I'm not the mom you need."

"Of course you are," I mumbled. I wished I was the kid she and Dad needed. I wished I were as independent as they thought I was. I wished I didn't need them. I wished I wasn't jealous of bugs and bison. I pushed down the feelings, but I couldn't push away a question.

The question, always buried in my mind, bloomed to the surface and wouldn't budge. A rogue mayfly zipped around the car interior, and I lowered my window to let it out before speaking. Watching it leave, I whispered, "Do you wish I would've died? So you and Dad could keep going on your trips and research and never have to deal with me?"

I didn't turn toward Mom. I couldn't. But I heard her breath suck in. Before she could answer me, I added, "Or maybe it would've been better if I hadn't been born at all?"

Mom grabbed me, her thin arms crushing me against her, holding me together even though she fell apart. Sobs erupted out of her. "I thank God every moment of every day for you, Ryder. Every single day. That you're here, that you're alive. It's the closest thing to a miracle I've ever seen. I don't just mean that your cancer is gone. I mean you."

She buried her head into my shoulder and soon my T-shirt was wet with her tears.

I wanted to cry, too. But I didn't.

"Thanks for taking me along tonight," I said.

"Thank you for coming along."

Mom put the car back into drive and slowly merged back onto the empty highway. I had just started drifting off when Mom said, "When was your last visit with Dr. Carpenio? It's almost a year, right?"

I didn't open my eyes and concentrated on breathing steadily so she thought I was asleep.

Chapter Nineteen

I'm a man, right? And men don't shake when they're scared.

So I wasn't exactly *shaking* Monday as I walked into school. I was trembling.

Okay, trembling sounds even worse than shaking. Fine. I was quaking. Scratch that. Even worse. Whatever. My body was having trouble not moving in miniscule amounts in all directions at once, which might have had something to do with knowing I'd be facing Max.

I thought I'd run into him before homeroom, since he usually hangs around Jocelyn's locker with her until the bell rings. But the hallway was clear. Maybe the Lord, in his infinite mercy, bestowed upon Max a virus! Or maybe he was too hurt to be here. Shame mingled with fear in my quivering body. Then I remembered that he broke up with Jocelyn, which explained the whole not being by her locker thing.

I have to admit, I was relieved that Jocelyn seemed absent that day, too.

I stood outside the cafeteria doors at lunchtime, no longer shaking. Not that I wasn't still freaking out a bit. I just think my body had given up on the whole shaking thing. After the lunch bell, I had made a pit stop by my locker. If Max was in school today, I'd see him in the cafeteria at what was now my usual table. Where would I sit? I went to the bathroom. And swung by the library to check the new releases. But there were still fifteen minutes left of lunch and all that trembling made for an empty stomach. I took a deep breath and pushed open the cafeteria doors.

Max sat in his usual seat with his back to where I stood. I knew he knew I was there because all around him, everyone sat up straight. Logan nudged him with his elbow and tilted his head in my direction. Here's the thing: I could've walked the far way around the table but I rushed straight ahead to the lunch line, wanting to get there fast as I could, even though it took me right by them.

I almost made it, too. But then someone kicked out a chair. I think it was Max. And not his usual, "Hey, have a seat buddy" kick. This time the chair was kicked *into* me. Of course I never saw it coming since Artie was on their side. Picture me, all right? Chair out of nowhere knocks my leg but I'm in such a scaredy-cat rush I can't stop my forward momentum. I do a funky half-split thing over the chair. I feel a ripping pain that I think is my jeans splitting down the back, but it's really just my pride (and maybe my butt a little, too, but don't picture that too much, okay?). I land in a sprawled out dumped-from-the-heavens heap on the sticky linoleum floor. (This next part, I'm pretty sure, happened in slow motion, so picture accordingly.) My head lands on top of my elbow. But just the edge of my face hits the elbow. The right side of my face, of course. The bit of face being my eye socket. Knocking Artie straight out of my head. It whips across the room, skidding to a stop under a table of cheerleaders. Painted-on-iris up, of course, making it seem I was somehow gazing up their skirts.

Brilliant.

By now you're nearly fifty thousand words into this little tale I'm sharing. By now you might've taken it upon yourself to do a little research on the one-eyed among you. Maybe you found out that that a fake eyeball isn't the round marble pirate shows would have you believe. They're more almond-shaped and mostly flat, sort of like a river stone. Making it pretty darn easy to kick from one side of the cafeteria to the other. I'm not even really faulting the cheerleader. Maybe she reacted on instinct. But she gave Artie a swipe with her foot as she screamed.

It flew to another table, where the next person screamed and kicked. And so on. And so on. A bunch of kids jumped up on their seats like it was a rabid mouse instead of an eyeball, pointing and screaming as it flew across the floor. More held their stomachs and a couple (for real) rolled on the floor laughing. I couldn't see the eye; it was much too small. But it was easy enough for the fully sighted to follow, so I knew about where it was from the way people pointed and screamed as it passed. Some people filmed the whole thing with their phones.

What was I doing this whole time? Well, it took way longer than it should've to stand up from the floor. When I finally did, the few kids who weren't actively watching my eye shoot across the room (or, of course, kicking my eye) were staring at me.

Because what's more fascinating than a fake eye being hockey pucked across the cafeteria? Catching a glimpse of the Cyclops himself.

I wasn't crying. I wasn't. I *wasn't*. But even though my eye isn't there, tear ducts are. Not having an eyeball suddenly makes tear ducts wig out a bit. That meant there was *drainage*, not tears, running down my cheeks.

"Aw, look at that!" some jerk said. "He's crying!"

"Ew! Can I see the socket?"

"Puke! Socket is such a shudder word! Get a picture!"

I pressed my hand over my eye. Okay, fine. I pressed my hand over where my eye was supposed to be. You're probably dying to know what an empty eye socket looks like (even though, like I said, at fifty thousand words or so, I'm a tad disappointed you didn't just look it up online). Maybe you think it's gooey and filled with pus. Maybe you think when I press my hand over it, it makes a sound akin to stirring a pot of mac-n-cheese. Man, you're sick. Actually, it's pretty boring. Just pink skin. Sort of like the inside of your nose, minus the nostril hair and snot, of course. Just skin. But it's, like, private.

What now, right? Hundreds of people kicking my eyeball around the room. Dozens staring at me. Teachers shouting for order. Tears—I mean *drainage*—running down my pathetic face. I wanted to run. But I needed my eye. I wanted to scream. But who would've listened? I wanted the floor to open up and swallow me. I needed a friend. But no one even *knew* me.

I—and if this isn't stupid, I don't know what is—turned all the way around so I could face Max Waters. If anyone could stop this, it was Papuaville Middle School's golden boy. Yet there was Max, laughing as hard as anyone. No splint on his nose or anything. Just a little bruise on the bridge.

Finally a roar split the room. "ENOUGH!" bellowed the fiercest voice I had ever heard. I whipped around again, and there was little round Miss Singer. Everyone froze. Everything froze. Except, of course, my eye, which landed with a soft smack into Miss Singer's practical plastic clog shoe. She bent down and picked it up. *Don't pass out. Don't pass out*, I mentally begged her. "Richie Ryder," she called, her voice still so loud it echoed. She held out Artie with a steady hand.

I was shaking all over again as I walked toward her. Suddenly the quiet of the room felt like moving through that mayfly swarm. Everyone was watching me, ready for me to crumble. A churning stew of horrible pain, rage, humiliation, and self-pity boiled in my gut, steaming up through my limbs. I wasn't sure I was going to make it to Miss Singer. I was going to erupt. I didn't want to see the people around me, but my stupid real eye wouldn't stop working. I'm pretty sure, in that moment, I'd have signed up for a dozen tumors in that eye rather than see faces shining with excitement, lips bit in shame, cheeks red with laughter, as I stumbled to Miss Singer.

And Miss Singer. Her face was the worst of all. Eyes wide and sad, mouth set in a straight line of fury. Her pity was so strong, it vibrated from her. It was tarry and thick, filling my lungs so my next breath quivered.

I wanted to grab that eye and run from the room. Run, and run, and run. Run back to Gramps's house. Or back to Addison. Or all the way to Alaska. *Run*, my mind cheered. *That's a good idea*. The wetness on my cheeks scalded suddenly and I knew it wasn't drainage any more.

The quiet—if it's possible—thickened when I reached out a trembling arm for my eye from Miss Singer. *This is it*, my mind beckoned. *Run!*

But I didn't.

I slammed a big old NOPE sign on the pain stew in my gut.

I climbed on top of a chair, standing high on shaking legs as everyone gasped around me. Cupping Artie in my palm, I spit on it, then rubbed it on the hem of my T-shirt.

"What are you doing, Richie Ryder?" Janet May squealed.

Holding up my empty socket with two fingers, I slowly, slowly, slowly popped the eye back into place. Then, arms out like this was all a huge theatrical joke, I bowed.

I bowed three times, in fact. One to the whole of the cafeteria (where everyone hooted and cheered), one to Miss Singer (who had turned a scary shade of green), and one to Max Waters (who probably chipped a molar with how hard he clenched his jaw).

I hopped down from the chair to thunderous applause. I made it all the way to the hall, too, before throwing up.

Even though the nurse sent me home from school, Gramps insisted I go to karate practice that night. "I've got plans," he stormed.

"I'll just stay home!"

"No way. The grief center people are meeting here. I'm making popcorn." Sure enough, a gold and black 1970s-era popcorn maker was on the kitchen table.

"I'll stay in my room, then!"

"You're going. That tournament is Saturday. You're going to need all the practice you can get."

Gramps didn't even turn off the car in the Waters Martial Arts parking lot—just stopped in front of the doors. Slowly, I got out. He pulled away before I could shut the door, making it slam on its own.

Neither Jocelyn nor Max were there. "What are you doing here?" Master Waters asked as I walked in.

"Practice," I said, confused.

"But the tournament is Saturday," Master Waters said, also confused. "Competitors rest up the week before tournaments so they don't get hurt. Sort of like Max and his broken nose." Master Waters's gaze snagged on the bruise blooming across my cheek from my fall in the cafeteria.

"It was an accident," I said, rubbing at the bruise.

"Those seem to be going around," Master Waters said. "Hope it's not serious. Max probably won't be able to go in the ring, thanks to that nose. If you want, you can go hang out with him at our house." He pulled his cell phone out of his pocket. "I'll let him know you're on your way."

"Ah, no!" I'm such a wordsmith sometimes. "That's okay. It's just, you said to train hard . . ."

"Yeah, go for a jog or something," Master Waters said. "I'm surprised the kids didn't mention anything to you at school today."

"It was sort of a crazy day."

"Right," Master Waters said. "Well, your mom paid the registration fee when she picked you up last week. Max handled all the registration paperwork, so you should be good to go. There are usually a lot of kids in your division, so rest up, son."

Maybe it was bug swarm talk, but when I texted Mom that karate class was canceled, I only had to wait a half-hour at the coffee shop across the street for her to pick me up. We even went to a diner for dinner, trying to give Gramps more time with his meeting. It was nice. Mom talked a lot about the mayflies. I saw her noticing the bruise on my cheek, too, but she didn't say anything. I mumbled something about falling in the cafeteria.

"You know, Ryder, if you want to talk, I'd love to listen."

"I know," I said. My phone buzzed. It was Dad.

"Go ahead," Mom said, even though we were still in the restaurant. When I got off the phone with Dad, I filled Mom in on what we had talked about (a baby bison was born that morning) and she didn't push for more details on how I fell.

When we finally arrived home, all the lights were off. There wasn't even the lingering smell of popcorn in the air. "How was your meeting?" I asked, sitting down on the nubby couch and ignoring the General's hiss. Mom had gone straight to bed.

Gramps shrugged.

"What?"

"All they want to talk about is moving on. Moving on. Like that's a good thing. *Gah.* I'm done with that group." He waved his hand like he was swatting bugs. "Oh, tell your mom some Dr. Cannoli or whatever called. I'm on your emergency contact list. Says he's been trying to set up an appointment."

I was spared having to respond to this by the doorbell ringing.

The General and I raced to the door. The General was a real cheat, trying to trip me for the second time that day. I kicked her off and hissed right back at her. Haughtily, she pranced down the hall to lick her butt.

Jocelyn stood in the doorway, a soft smile on her face.

I waited for the rush of warmth that I always got from the moment I first laid eye on her. The soaring, drenching heat that radiated from her smile to my chest. Nothing.

"Can I come in?" she asked.

"Of course." I stepped back to make room for her. Her bare arm brushed my forearm. No sparks. Not even a flicker. "Actually," I said, looking over my shoulder at where Gramps perched in his recliner like it was the throne of the Kingdom Crank, "let's go outside."

"I heard about what happened at school today," she said as we settled next to yard horse.

I shrugged. "No biggie."

Jocelyn scooted closer to me. I let my head fall onto her shoulder for a moment, waiting for the electricity to ignite again. It felt nice, don't get me wrong, but it wasn't like how it had been whenever we were near each other before. Once I figured everything out with Max . . . after the tournament . . . I was sure it'd be like it was.

Jocelyn turned so that she faced me. The moonlight shimmered in her dark hair. I ran the tips of my fingers through her hair, knowing it would feel silky and cool. Suddenly her mouth was pressed against mine.

Did I kiss her? Or did she kiss me? Did it even matter?

As we pulled apart, I was glad it didn't make one of those squelching smacking sounds you hear in movies. Then I was freaked out that *that* was my only thought. This was (believe it or not) my first kiss. Shouldn't I be feeling *something* other than being relieved it was over?

What was wrong with me?

"So, things are going to be weird at school, huh?" Jocelyn squeezed my hand.

"Yeah," I said. I lay on my back, slipping my hand out from under hers and resting my head on my folded hands. "I'm going to lie low for a while."

"I'll sit with you at lunch?" It was definitely a question, not a statement.

"Nah, the quilt club is pushing to finish a bunch of guinea pig squares in time for graduation gifts. I'm going to help out."

Jocelyn cocked an eyebrow at me. "Really?"

"What?" I shrugged. "It's a big project."

"And convenient."

Across the street, Jocelyn's mom opened the screen door and called for her.

"See you tomorrow," I said, not sitting up.

"Bye." But Jocelyn didn't get up right away. "Are you . . . are you upset with me? You seem kind of distant."

I sighed, still staring up at the night sky. "It's just been a bad day, that's all."

Chapter Twenty

I wasn't *dodging* anyone, okay? I actually had a stomach-ache when I woke up Tuesday. A real one, too, complete with a little upchuck. (Sorry if you're eating. But if you are eating, do me a solid and don't use the pages as a napkin. I put a lot of time into this story. I'd like it back when you're done.) Anyway, it was a legit sickness.

I spent the entire day on the nubby couch watching the Food Network with the General.

"I'm having a, um, meeting in the kitchen." Gramps stood in front of me, hair slicked back and shiny, and he was wearing a buttoned-down shirt and shiny dress shoes. The look would've been better if he hadn't also been wearing shorts instead of pants, but still, Gramps was looking fine.

I whistled low. "Gramps, you're stylin'."

His ears pinked. "*Pschaw*," he said, waving his hand like he was pushing my words away.

"I thought you were done with the grief group thing."

Gramps smoothed his slick hair with his palm. "Giving it one more try."

"Is Logan coming over?" Like I said, I wasn't dodging anyone, but if anyone from school was heading over . . .

"He's at school, doofus. Like you should be."

"Oh. I thought he'd be there for meetings."

"Logan just came up with the idea. The rest of us are making the group, keeping it to just adults, too. It has a name, you know," Gramps said. "We're calling it GAS. Grieving Adults Support."

"GAS? You're calling a group of old farts *gas*?"

Gramps winked at me. "My idea."

"Don't worry," I added as the doorbell rang. "I'll stay clear."

Gramps led Rosie, a cotton ball of a woman with frizzy white hair and a roundish body, past me to the kitchen while I took my third nap of the day. I only woke up when I heard the door slam shut.

"Are you okay?" I asked as Gramps stomped by.

"Just dandy," he grumped.

Stomachache returned Wednesday.

Stomachache Thursday, too.

"Stomach—"

"School or the doctor's?" Mom said Friday.

I picked school.

"I think I know what's going on here," Mom said after doing that Mom thing where she checked my temperature with her cheek.

"Great. Maybe you could explain it to me," I muttered.

"You're nervous about the karate tournament."

I groaned. Honestly? I had sort of forgotten about the tournament. Thanks, Mom, for the new worry.

"Don't be nervous, sweetie." Mom kissed my forehead. "You'll be fine. It's going to be a strange thing, cheering on your child as he fights another child. Sort of contrary to our hippie parenting. But I guess they don't give out trophies for hugging things out at martial arts tournaments."

"Does that mean you're planning on going?" I asked.

"Wouldn't miss it, kiddo."

I hung out in the quilt club room until about thirty seconds before the last bell for homeroom. As I was walking into school, I realized that the thread stockpile totally made more sense if organized in Roy G. Biv order, you know? My head throbbed like it had been quilted by the time I was done, but it felt good to bring some order to the club. Not that they'd appreciate it. Janet May already snarked that the alphabetical order she had institutionalized was just fine. Control freak, that one. Can you believe she accused me of trying to skirt running into Max in the hall, too? Totally untrue. I was avoiding Jocelyn, who was waiting for me in homeroom.

"Where've you been?" Jocelyn said as I slid into my seat.

"I've been sick."

"Too sick to return my texts?"

"I'm sorry," I whispered, meaning it. I thought about telling her I also ignored about fifty texts from Alice. I was an equal opportunity ignorer.

After bio, Miss Singer called me to her desk just as Jocelyn turned to me. I shrugged. "Catch up with you later."

Jocelyn bit her lip. "We have a lot to talk about."

"I know."

Jocelyn looked down, her dark hair covering her eyes. Without thinking, I swept it back with my fingertips.

Jocelyn smiled in response, and for some reason that made me feel worse.

"Mr. Raymond," Miss Singer snapped as I approached her desk. "Are you okay?"

"Yeah," I said, realizing too late I was flapping my hand the way Gramps does. I let my hand drop. "Just a stomach bug, I guess."

Miss Singer nodded. "Nothing to do with what happened on Monday?"

"What happened on Monday?" I asked, like I couldn't remember. "Oh, you mean in the cafeteria—with Artie?" I flapped my hand again. "That was nothing. Guys have been high-fiving me all morning. It was hilarious!"

She nodded again. "Are you using the notebook I gave you?"

I didn't say anything.

"If you'd like to talk to someone, I'm here. But if you want a professional, our school counselor is excellent—"

"I'm *good*," I snapped.

Saturday morning, I woke up to a note waiting for me on the kitchen table. *Something urgent came up, Ryder. Gramps will take you to the tournament and I'll meet you there.*

"Wouldn't miss it, huh, Mom?"

"You talking to yourself, boy?" Gramps tied a black and white bandana around his head like the old Asian guy in the first *Karate Kid* movie. I had a sinking suspicion the yard horse had a matching ensemble. He clapped his hands together and rubbed them. "Let's go!"

I switched out my usual so-sad-even-plastic-trees-make-me-miserable playlist to something more upbeat to get into the right fighting frame of mind as we drove down the block. Then I gave up entirely when Gramps jammed to this epic '70s tune with all these trumpets and clarinets that made my heart wiggle in my chest. He bopped along so hard that the Oldsmobile rocked.

"Come on, kid!" he yelled. "If this song was good enough for Rocky, it's good enough for you!"

"Good enough for who?"

"*Pschaw!*" Hand flap.

I have to admit, by the end of the song I might've been hooting an imaginary jazz clarinet. We were laughing too hard when the song finished to realize the next one was a total downer. Some dweeb singing way too sincerely about liking to dream. I fake puked at the next lyric, about holding each other in paradise until he wakes. Then I saw Gramps, his goofy grin gone, replaced with twisting, shaking lips.

"Haven't heard this song in a long time." His voice was thick. "Go ahead, change it, Richie Ryder."

I almost did, and had my hand on the knob to change the station and everything. Then I said, "Nah. I like it."

Gramps nodded. "Your grandma liked it, too." He smiled. "She was the happiest person you'd ever met but listened to the saddest drivel you can imagine."

"Hey—I do that, too!" I said.

"How 'bout that," Gramps murmured, a smile still on his face.

The tournament venue was about an hour away and my stupid chest didn't start freaking out until we pulled into the packed parking lot. Tons of martial artists poured into the building, many of them holding weapons—long swords, evil-looking curved blades, wooden staffs. Others had uniforms that looked more like what you'd expect a boxer to wear, all silky and shiny. Granted, a bunch were skinny and scared looking, too, but most carried themselves like nothing—and no one—could touch them.

For a minute or two, Gramps and I just stared. "You better get moving," he finally said, and pointed to the glowing red clock on the dashboard. The tournament was going to start in five minutes. "Don't you have to register or something?"

"No, just need to check in. Max handled the registration." Honestly, just thinking of Max brought my nerves to a whole new threshold of what-the-heck-are-you-doing-here.

Gramps clapped a hand on my shoulder. "Either you win or you get your butt kicked," he said.

"Great pep talk, Gramps."

He dropped his arm to take the key out of the ignition. "Either way," he continued, "you've done something great. You put yourself out there, and that's the scariest thing."

I waited for the punchline, but it never came.

Picture the tournament: an enormous gymnasium broken up into ten rings. By ring, I mean a square mat with judges stationed in each corner. After I signed in, the registration person handed me an index card with the number of my ring (7) and a schedule. First up were weapons, then sparring. So I had some time to kill.

"You sure this is your ring?" Gramps asked as we made our way to the bleachers in front of ring 7.

I double checked the card. "Yeah, this is it."

The bleachers were packed, and the ring was too far away for me to make out the martial artists going through their weapons forMs. (Just so you know: no one fights with weapons. Man, that'd be a show, huh?

Each person just does a form with the weapons. If they drop their weapons at any point, they're automatically disqualified.)

A groan and then a smattering of applause broke out from in front of the ring. "Aw, man. Someone dropped their weapon, huh?" I said to Gramps.

He just nodded, eyes on the ring.

"Hey—you look worried," I said to him. "I got this!"

Gramps's eyes slid to mine, then back to the ring. "Who was it that registered you here? Master Waters?"

"No, Max."

"Huh."

"What?"

"Nothing," Gramps said after too long a pause. "There's your team." He pointed to a cluster of people walking through the doors. I recognized the white and black uniforms, got up, and hurried toward them. (I know what you're thinking: *Hurrying* toward *them? The people you've been avoiding all week?* Here's the thing: maybe all the jazz clarinet scrambled my brain, but something Gramps said in the car triggered a need to talk to Max. That thing about the scariest part being actually putting yourself out there.) I ran into Master Waters first, as he walked away from Jocelyn and Max. "Ready to go, Mr. Raymond?"

"Yes, sir."

"Good, good. School's counting on you and Jocie, too, since Max can't compete." He crossed his arms and glared at me.

"Ah." I took a deep breath. "Well, I'll be at ring seven, okay?" I tried to scoot around him.

"Seven?" Master Waters echoed.

I nodded, hurrying after Max.

He and Jocelyn were whisper fighting. Not good. *Put yourself out there.* I stepped closer to them. Jocelyn turned to me, pressing a hand into my chest. Max turned away. "Jocelyn, can I have a minute to talk with Max?"

"Ryder," she whispered, "maybe we should talk first . . ."

"No, I really need to talk to him."

Jocelyn sighed. "All right. Come find me after, okay? I need to sign in still anyway."

I nodded without really looking at her. Max found a seat on the edge of piled up mats beside the bleachers. Up close now, I could see the faint bruising under his eyes. His nose looked a little swollen but not much. The way his face was twisted, though, and the way his shoulders slumped, he looked like he was in major pain.

"I'm sorry about your nose." My words rushed out before I wimped out of saying it. "I don't know why I hit you. I shouldn't have. It's like, you . . . you make me see everything that's wrong with me. Everything I don't want to see." I half-snorted. "And I already can't see a lot, so that's something."

Max didn't react, just kept glaring at his feet.

"Anyway, I shouldn't have done it." I heard my voice harden. "And you shouldn't have done what you did to me in the cafeteria." Again I paused, but he didn't so much as flinch.

"I didn't do anything in the cafeteria. You tripped," he spoke in a whisper.

I shook my head. "I tripped on the chair you kicked into me."

Max shrugged. "How was I supposed to know your eye would fall out?"

"You weren't," I said. "But when it did, you could've stopped what happened next. You know you could've. If you had just—"

"Just what?" Max asked.

"Told them to stop. They would've listened to you. Everyone listens to you. You're like the hometown hero." My stomach twisted, remembering how he had sat there in the cafeteria. The way he was just sitting there now. "So we're even."

"Even?" Max grunted. When he looked up at me, I stepped back at the twisted, hate-filled look he threw my way. He laughed, but it was bitter. "You punch me, then

259

you steal my girlfriend, and you think we're even because I didn't stop other people from picking on you?"

"Well, it sounds a little one-sided when you put it that way." I laughed nervously. Max didn't. "And I didn't steal your girlfriend. Jocelyn said you broke up with her."

"Then you're not with Jocelyn?" Max looked up, staring at me.

"Wait? What? We're not . . . it's not like that." I mean, yeah, we kissed. But it wasn't like she was my girlfriend or anything.

"You didn't make a move on her less than an hour after we broke up?" Max spit out.

"No, of course not." Because it wasn't like, *a move.* Somehow we kissed. But I didn't kiss her. It just happened.

Max jumped to his feet. "You know, I always try to do what's right. But with you? I just can't. And now—you standing here, lying straight to my face? I don't even feel bad about it. We're not even. Not even close." He leaned in. I felt his hot breath on my face. "Yet." His eyes flicked to the rings. "Better suit up. Your ring is ready."

Jocelyn ran up to me as I made my way to ring 7. She smiled, and for just a moment, I felt the flicker of that old electricity. I grinned back. So it hadn't gone as I had hoped (honestly, I sort of pictured that whole exchange with Max ending with fist bumps and maybe a pep talk or something), but I hadn't dodged something that scared me, and that felt pretty good.

"How'd that go? When I told Max we were together, he didn't—"

"What? Why would you say that?"

Jocelyn's cheeks flushed. "Because we sort of are."

I backed up a step. "Listen, Jocelyn. I like you. I do. But let's just slow down a minute."

"Are you serious?" Jocelyn's voice pitched. "You made how you felt pretty darn clear again and again when I was with Max. Now I'm not with him and you want to *slow down*?"

"Well, yeah." I grabbed my hair in a fist.

Jocelyn stared at me. Her eyes were wide and hurt. She looked delicate as a doll (if, you know, a doll could whup my butt in five seconds flat). Her lip trembled. I wanted to hug her. I wanted to tell her it would be okay. I wanted to kiss her and tell her she was beautiful and that I was a wreck and I didn't deserve her. More than anything—I wanted to *want* to be her boyfriend. But I didn't.

I didn't feel anything.

"Something is wrong with me," I whispered.

Over the loudspeaker, the announcer cut in: "All sparring contestants, report to your rings. Competition is about to begin!"

I half stepped toward Jocelyn, who took a full step back. "Go." So I walked away without even wishing her good luck.

At ring 7, I grabbed my duffel bag and put on my sparring gear. I looked around for Gramps in the bleachers but didn't see him. I didn't see Mom, either, which made me feel even worse. Where was she? A judge, wearing a martial arts uniform and a master belt (black with a red stripe through the center), asked for my card. He studied it and then squinted at me. "Okay," he said after a minute, "you're up first."

I jammed the helmet on and lowered the face shield as I stood in the ring, bouncing on my toes, thinking through what Master Waters had told me about the tournament. The first person to get three hits or kicks wins. Head contact was allowed. Kicks only counted above the waist. *Be first*, Master Waters had told me. *But don't forget dodging.* I closed my eyes and mentally ran through some combos I wanted to try—roundhouse-rib jab-side kick was my favorite.

Just as I was trying to get my game face on, I registered Gramps and Master Waters yelling about something to the side of the ring. I opened my eyes to see the judge and my opponent in front of me. Only my opponent wasn't exactly standing. He was about my age, maybe a year or two older. His arms were enormous; this guy could totally knock me out. But his legs were skinny. Probably not much of a kicker. Considering, you know, that he was in a wheelchair.

"What's going on?" I looked around. Master Waters was pointing at me and yelling at the person who took my registration. That guy was holding up his hands and shaking his head. Gramps wasn't yelling anymore. He simply looked over at me and shrugged.

"Fighters, begin!" the judge called.

I looked at the guy I was supposed to fight. The guy in a wheelchair. My fighting stance (hands up, one leg bent slightly at the knee and in front of the other) dropped. My opponent's jaw clenched and he glared at me. "Come on!" he yelled.

"I can't." I backed up.

But it wasn't fast enough. Because this guy—somehow he made that wheelchair fly. He jumped—I'm serious!—wheelchair and all and slammed into me. His ridge hand knocked me so hard the face shield splintered. All I saw were jagged cracks.

"Hey!" I snapped.

"Point!" the judge called.

"Call the match!" Master Waters yelled.

I pulled off the helmet as Master Waters stepped onto the mat. "There's been a mistake. Mr. Raymond shouldn't be in the special needs division. There was a registration error."

"Hey!" the registration guy called from the sidelines. "Mistake? Your school signed him up for this division. Not us!"

"What?" I asked. "What's going on?"

Gramps waved me to the side of the mat. The guy I was fighting made his way over, too. "Max signed you up as special needs," Gramps said. Something flickered in his eyes. Was it pity? "Might've been a mistake."

"It was no mistake," I said, thinking of Max's warning that we weren't even *yet*.

The guy I had been fighting cough-laughed. "Man," he said. "Some kid signs you up as special needs to humiliate you, then you go and get your butt handed to you by a guy in a wheelchair. That sucks, dude."

"I'm—I didn't mean . . ."

"Nah, it's cool." The guy held out a fist.

I bumped it. "I'm Richie." Gramps nudged me with his elbow. I'm not sure why I said Richie instead of Ryder. It just slipped out.

"Nate," the guy said. "Sorry about your face shield."

"It's okay. I hate wearing it anyway."

"Why don't you just get a usual helmet?" Nate asked. "I mean, you'd have a shiner now, but you're not going to face anyone as good as me in the *normal* division."

"Dude, no one is normal," I said. "I've got to wear this to protect my eye. The other is a fake."

"That sucks, Richie," Nate said as he wheeled away.

My actual division—the one I should have been registered for—was just beginning in ring 5. Master Waters was already there, reaming out Max. "I trusted you, kid. You let me down. You let your team down."

Max didn't say anything.

"I'm sorry, son," Master Waters said. "You're off the team. I can't give you special treatment."

Max still didn't say anything.

"We'll discuss this later. Jocelyn is about to go on the mat. Are you coming to cheer her on, or what?"

Max tilted his head at the mat. "I'll stay here. For Ryder."

Master Waters nodded. "That's a good step in the right direction."

This division was a lot bigger. Already there were two kids fighting on the mat and three more of us waiting. I tried to block out Max watching from the side, Gramps trying to round up a different face shield, and the noise of Jocelyn's division a few rings away. And where the heck was Mom? She said she'd be here! I tried to concentrate only on the fighters I'd be facing, taking note of the way one kid did nothing but side kick—I'd sidestep and roundhouse him—and another blitzed from the second the match began—whirling out in an explosion of punches. It was a good move but it only worked once, and this guy was doing it every time he fought. If I faced him, I'd stop him with a well-timed side kick.

Everything else—the messed up feelings with Jocelyn, Max declaring himself my mortal enemy, even the stuff with my eye and school and Gramps and Mom and Dad and . . . everything. Everything melted away. It was just me, getting ready to fight.

For a second, something flared inside of me, which was directed at Max. That he would take this escape away from me, making it about what was wrong with my body instead of what it could do, sizzled inside me. I tamped down the fury and concentrated on the sparring instead.

Finally my name was called just as Gramps ran up to me. "Sorry, Richie," he said. "I can't find another face shield."

Max snorted from the sidelines.

I shrugged, ripping the remnants of my shield from where it plugged into my helmet, and suddenly was glad Mom wasn't around after all. "I'll go without it."

"You can't, doofus. One eye, remember? Protect the spare and all that." Gramps flapped his hand at me. "You didn't even bring your glasses."

I ignored him, stepping onto the mat at the same time as my opponent. This guy had a couple inches on me and was super thin like a whip. He looked fast. And cocky, considering he winked at me as we shook hands.

"Remember to protect your right!" Max called. For a second, I thought maybe he actually did feel guilty, enough so to start coaching me again. "You're totally blind to the right. If he tries to hit you there, you're screwed!"

Nope. Not even. He was just being a jerk.

The judge pointed to Max. "Any more specific pointers like that and you're out of here." Turning to us, he said, "Fighters ready? Begin!"

Sure enough, the kid sent a flurry of roundhouse kicks to my right. Thanks, Max, for that little heads-up. I twisted and blocked, whipping away his leg and pegging him in the ribs. The judge stopped the match and awarded me the point.

Two more to go.

"Sweep the leg!" Gramps yelled, then folded over laughing at himself. "*Cah, cah, cah!*"

Almost immediately, the guy whapped me in the shoulder. "Point!"

I borrowed the blitz tactic and landed a jab in the chest, practically pushing the guy off the mat. This time, I winked at him as I was awarded another point.

One more to go.

Two things happened at once. First—and it took a while to believe my eye on this—Mom and Dad rushed to the ringside. That's right: Mom *and* Dad. Second thing: Max shouted out more helpful advice. "Remember, if you get knocked in your left eye, you're totally screwed!"

"Fighters, begin!" the judge called.

"Dad?" I said.

Bam! Ridge hand to my left eye.

Chapter Twenty-One

I *don't want* to be dramatic about this.

But that hit to the eye?

It took about a thousand years to fall to the mat, Mom's screams still echoing in my skull. For a moment, I could see—Dad rushing toward me, Max's face filled with shame, Gramps bellowing—then blackness. Blackness forever.

Naw. I'm just kidding.

What really happened was this: I got knocked in the eye. It watered like crazy.

"Stop the fight! Stop the fight!" Mom screamed as Dad ran straight across the mat and grabbed me.

He held my face in his hands. "Good to see you, son."

"You too, Dad."

"Well, you won't see me for long. That's about to swell shut." Dad shook his head at me and slowly the amount that I could see diminished to about a sliver.

"Ice! We need ice!" Mom yelled.

Then, of course, everything went black as a judge pressed an ice pack to my eye. "Will we be able to resume the fight soon?"

"No," Mom snapped. To me, she added, "Where was your face shield?"

"It shattered in my first fight so I went without it."

"I'm going to kill you, Richie Ryder Raymond." Mom pulled me into her. Apparently, the murdering would be after the hugging.

Here's the truth: Dr. Carpenio can lecture like no other.

"We agreed that you'd be monitored annually. That's once a year. Once a year. Yet I haven't seen you in almost twenty months. Do you understand why we monitor you so closely? Do you all understand what's at stake for Ryder?"

"I'm back to being Richie now," I cut in. Everyone ignored me.

"Of course, we understand what's at stake," Dad broke in. "His remaining vision. His . . . life. We get it. We messed up."

"We just lost track of time," Mom added.

"My office left no less than four messages for you on your cell and home phone," Dr. Carpenio said.

"What? I never got any of those," Mom said, the shock apparent in her voice.

I squirmed in my seat, somehow feeling all of their eyes on me and sort of wishing my left eye was still swollen shut. But the tournament had been two days earlier and I could actually see Dad's outraged face, Mom's hurt expression. (By the way, that "something urgent" that came up? It was Dad getting an earlier flight home as a surprise.)

"Richie?" Mom snapped.

"I might've deleted one or two—"

"Why would you do that?" she gasped.

After the longest thirty seconds of silence ever, Dr. Carpenio broke in, his tone much gentler. "I'm sure he did it for the same reason you didn't put more effort into tracking the appointments. You were scared. Scared what we'd find when we did have another screening. I get that." He sighed. "But the fact is, you have a chronic condition, Ryder. I mean, Richie. And you, Dr. Raymond and . . ." he nodded to my dad, ". . . Dr. Raymond, you have a child with a chronic condition. It's scary, sure. But that's life. Get over it. Take care of business."

I got why Dr. Carpenio was super grouchy. I mean, Mom did pull the fellow-doctor card and begged a last-minute Saturday appointment, calling Dr. Carpenio on his cell phone and saying she couldn't trust anyone but him. And Dr. Carpenio *did* arrange for an emergency MRI and rushed bloodwork that Saturday. Now we were gathered at his office to hear the results. And to get a lecture, of course.

"Well," Dr. Carpenio sighed, "I've got news."

"Good news or bad news?" Mom asked.

Did your hands ever sweat so suddenly it felt like they were melting? I used to think this feeling in my stomach at this point of every doctor's visit was like being punched in the gut. Then I took up martial arts, and I now know that this feeling is much, much worse than a simple punch in the gut. I pushed around thoughts about my recent headaches, of having to get closer to things than I was used to, of what it was like to go through radiation. For a stupid second, I almost bolted from the room.

"Both," Dr. Carpenio said, still looking at his files. "First, the bad news: you're going to need new glasses. Real glasses, this time. You have a refractive error but it's easy enough to correct. With glasses, I'm confident we can bring your vision back up to twenty-seventy. Maybe even better."

"Wait?" Dad said. "That's the bad news?"

"Yes," Dr. Carpenio smiled. "The good news is that you're not showing any form of disease. Bloodwork, MRI, exam—everything is normal. That's not to say that you can skip your next screening, of course."

"Of course," I gushed, breathing for what felt like the first time in a year.

Here's the part that sucks as much as it was amazing: Mom's relieved tears over her crinkled-paper face hollowed me just as fast as the smile on Dad's sunshine face filled me up.

Everything was normal.

After the doctor's appointment, we all went to dinner at this restaurant that had an arcade, and we spent a couple hours and way too much of Mom and Dad's money playing racing games. On the way home, we stopped at a roadside stand for ice cream, which made me feel like a little kid, but it was nice.

Dad and I were still working on our ice cream cones—rocky road for him, birthday bash for me—when Mom ditched her black raspberry swirl for coffee flavored. She always does that, trying at least a few flavors before she settles on which she likes most. Sort of reminds me of a fly, flitting from plate to plate.

Dad turned toward me with his face drawn into the first serious expression any of us wore since Dr. Carpenio's office, and I guessed the two of them plotted Mom's sudden need for another cone.

"Ryder," he said.

"Richie," I corrected. Dad sort of flinched.

"I haven't been here, not like I should've been." Dad stared at his melting ice cream but didn't eat it, not even as it dripped down his hand. "I don't just mean because of work. I mean, as a father. I'm not . . . I'm not so good at it."

"Dad—"

"No, Richie, listen. It should be so easy, you know. So normal and natural. But it isn't for me. I love you, kid. Completely love you an almost frightening amount, but I'm not—"

"Dad," I interrupted a little louder, "I get it. Gramps, he told me about how when your mom died he sort of shut down. You didn't exactly have a great role model. But it's cool. We're good."

"No, we're not." Dad shook his head. His ice cream had totally dissolved, covering his hand in muddy-looking rivers. He took a deep breath. "We're going to change things. I mean it. Mom said there are spots at the Natural History Museum for researchers like me. I'll be local and—no arguing about this—we're going to have to figure out how to deal with things instead of running or ignoring them. Maybe get some help—"

I had to put the big guy out of his misery. "All right."

"Thanks, Ry . . . Richie." Dad let out a long breath and flicked some of his melted ice cream off his hand onto the grass surrounding our picnic table.

I licked around my cone, thinking about Miss Singer and the notebook she carried around. The blank one she gave me. "My bio teacher, she says she writes down her . . . feelings. Maybe I should do that. She seems pretty normal."

Dad nodded. "That's a great idea." He took a deep breath. "Your mom thinks we should hook you up with a therapist, too. Now, don't argue—"

"Cool," I said. "I think that'd be nice."

The sun was setting by the time we pulled into the driveway. I saw the curtain flick in the front window of the house. "Did anyone let Gramps know? You know, about my results?"

"Oh!" Mom said. "I didn't think . . ."

"I'm sure the old man's fine," Dad said, with a nonchalant air.

I remembered what Gramps said about the day Marlene told him she was sick. About how he remembered every detail. Had he been thinking about that all day, because of me? I pushed the thought aside.

"Hey, Gramps!" I said as I stepped over the General on the way inside. "Cancer-free!"

"Oh." He was in his recliner now, all the way pushed back like he hadn't just been peeking out the window, flipping through the channels. A shudder moved across his face but only for a second. "That's good."

Mom sat down on the other chair and I plopped on the couch, which finally had some give to it. The General hopped onto my lap. Either the cat was starting to like me or she figured this was the best way to keep tabs on my movements. I rubbed her behind the ears and she latched, her back legs ripping up my arm. Definitely the latter, then.

Dad sat on the edge of the narrow couch beside me. Funny, you know? He grew up in this house. It hadn't changed a bit. Yet he was the one who looked uncomfortable being here.

"What's the plan now?" Gramps asked.

"Well," Dad said, "I finished the field aspect of my project. Now I'm going to launch into publishing papers, which can be done anywhere. Jenna's going to help set me up with some place in DC, like her, for a while. I suppose we'll find a home nearby to settle for a few months."

"Wait! What?" I asked. "We *can't* move." Gramps's face turned toward mine for just a second, then back to the TV. "I've—I've got school . . ."

276

"We'll stay local until you finish the school year, Ry—Richie," Dad said.

Mom didn't say anything, her eyes flicking between me and Gramps. "What would you like to do, Richie?"

"Can't we stay here?" I asked.

"You know your gramps. He's stuck in his ways," Dad said, like Gramps wasn't sitting a couple feet away. "He doesn't want us hanging around indefinitely."

"Gramps?" I asked.

But the old man just got up and walked back to his bedroom like I never spoke.

"See?" Dad said. He grabbed the remote control from Gramps's recliner. And I felt sick to my stomach.

Much later—after Mom and Dad had gone to dinner and a movie—I started to lose the whole not-going-to-die-yet good vibe and remembered that not all was fine in the life of Richie Ryder Raymond.

I had the girl I crushed on all year calling me "boyfriend" and suddenly I wasn't all that sure I liked her that way anymore.

I had the guy who cared about everyone hating my guts.

And I had the ongoing issue of, you know, Artie.

Forget it, I told myself. Soon we'd be moving and that would eliminate problems one and two. But I couldn't push the feelings away, no matter how hard I tried. It was like they banged around inside of me. *Bam! Bam! Bam!*

Too slowly I realized the banging I heard wasn't coming from inside me. It was coming from the front yard. I pushed open the screen door to see Gramps. Next to him was a bucket full of tools. He held a huge hammer with two hands. *Bam! Bam! Bam!* Gramps started beating the crap out of the yard horse.

"What are you doing?" I ran to his side, keeping a few feet between me and the hammer.

Bam! Bam! Bam!

"What do you care? You're leaving!" *Bam! Bam!*

"Gramps, what is going *on*?"

The clouds shifted, letting moonlight shine on Gramps's face. Huge tears slid down his wrinkled cheeks and for a second I couldn't breathe. "Gramps?"

"Set in my ways," he grumbled. "Maybe I don't want to be set in my ways. Ever think of that? Maybe I just push things away so much that the ways get stuck. I get stuck. Worse than a stupid stone horse." *Bam! Bam! Bam!* "Dress it up all you like. Make it a joke. It's still stuck." A chunk of concrete fell from the horse's shoulder. "That one eye'll fall out if you keep staring, boy. Leave me alone."

I almost did, too. Instead, I pulled another hammer out of the bucket. I slammed it against the horse, feeling the jolt of the impact up my arm. I slammed the hammer down again and again, on the other side of Gramps. It felt like each hit was cracking me to pieces. Maybe it was. At least, it splintered the parts of me I glued together myself—the parts that dammed up everything I didn't want to feel. With each thud of the hammer on that stone horse, anger roared through me. Pain. Pity. *Bam! Bam! Bam!*

"I hate horses. Freaky beasts with freaky bulgy eyes," Gramps huffed. "Stop!" he suddenly yelled at me. He rooted in the bucket for a second and handed me a pair of goggles. I slid them up my nose.

"I hate goggles!" *Slam! Slam!* "I hate glasses! I hate my stupid, freaky fake eye!" *Slam! Slam! Slamslamslamslam!*

"I hate going to bed alone." *Bam!* "I hate waking up. Forty years and I still think she's going to be there on the other side of the bed." *Bam! Bam! Bam!*

A bit of the horse's tail crumbled. Gramps moved onto the face.

I pulled back, holding the hammer with two hands and slamming into the yard horse's hindquarters. "I hate needing help!" *Slam!* "I hate being different!" *Slam!*

"I'm tired of being a joke!" *Bam! Bam!*

More pieces crumbled.

"I miss seeing stars every night," I said softer, but hitting the horse harder.

"I miss her laugh." Another chunk crumbled.

Vaguely, I realized Jocelyn was standing there in the grass. I guess breaking apart a stone horse can wake up the neighbors.

"Hey, *neigh*bor," I joked. *Bam! Bam! Bam!* "I hate puns!"

Gramps laughed. A bit of the horse's nose crumbled. "I want to date again. I like Rosie, darnit."

Bam! Bam! I wanted to raise my arms and hit the horse again, but my limbs suddenly weighed a thousand pounds. "I'm tired of being funny."

"Ah, you were never that funny, really."

"Oh thanks, Gramps."

Jocelyn stared at us for a minute. She picked up a wrench from the bucket.

"Go for it," Gramps said, pointing to the side of the horse opposite me.

I whacked the horse again. "It's not fair," I grunted. Then I hit it again, harder. I was a volcano, a tornado, a hurricane. "It's not fair!" I yelled to the stupid horse. To the stars. To the world. "I just want to be normal!"

A strangled sort of whimper escaped from Jocelyn. For a second, I thought maybe she had hit her thumb or something, but she kept right on swinging at the horse, too. "It was raining," she said. *Slam!*

"They gave me ice cream after," I grunted. *Bam!*

Gramps sat in the grass, his head in his hands.

"It was my idea to light the heater." *Slam!*

"I'm scared all the time." *Bam!*

"It's my fault he's dead." *Slam!*

"I'll never not be scared." *Bam!*

"I'll never be okay." *Slam!*

I don't know how long we pelted that stone horse, but by the time we collapsed next to Gramps, whole chunks of it had crumbled to the grass. But we weren't able to knock it over. We lay in a triangle, faces staring up at the sky and covered in sweat.

I couldn't push back what was in me. It was too close to the surface now. Too real. I was too tired to fight it, though. So I just felt it. I let the fear and anger and self-pity roll through me. It sucked. I'm just being honest, here. It felt just as awful as I always thought it would. But maybe it was hearing Gramps's quiet sobs next to me and feeling that electricity zapping again between where Jocelyn lay, out of breath, on the other side of me, letting me know I wasn't alone—that they were just as wrecked as I was.

Somehow I knew they'd be all right. Even though they felt as pelted to pieces as me—as that stupid yard horse—I *knew* they'd be okay. And if they'd be okay, well . . . maybe I'd be okay, too.

Yes, I'd be okay.

A piece of the horse fell to the grass behind us.

Quietly I heard Jocelyn's voice: "It was raining so we couldn't go to the fort. We went to the shed instead. It was cold, though, in the rain. I had dandelions. I said we should make them into tea, that it's something Indians would've done."

"You'll be okay."

"I knocked over the heater," Jocelyn whispered. "*I* got scared and hid instead of leaving. *I'm* why he's dead."

"You're wrong," a gruff voice over us said. There was Max. Maybe everyone else had seen him walking up, or maybe they were just too tired to be surprised by his appearing there, seemingly out of nowhere. I looked around for Master Waters's Jeep, but then remembered Max only lived a couple blocks from us.

"I came to apologize to Ryder," Max said, even as he kept his eyes on Jocelyn, who hadn't moved. "You don't remember, Jocie, do you? *I* lit the heater. And then I ran when it fell. I *ran*, yet everyone thinks I'm some kind of hero."

All three of us went up on our elbows as Max spoke. Gramps sighed and pushed himself to his feet. He walked over to Max and put his hammer in Max's hand. "People die. They die in horrible, awful ways sometimes. Maybe even a little bit at a time. It's not fair. But it's not anyone's fault." Gramps tilted his head toward the horse.

"Go ahead," I urged. "Beat up the yard horse. It'll make you feel better."

Jocelyn nodded, then lay back down. I followed suit.

"I'm tired of being perfect." Max hit the horse.

"I'm tired of being messed up," Jocelyn whispered. Then she screamed it. "I'm tired of being messed up!"

Max slammed the hammer again. "I'm *glad* I'm off the team."

Jocelyn stood. She held out her hand and pulled me to my feet. She took a deep breath, raising her arms over her head. "I'm tired of hiding my scars." She swept off her big sweatshirt so she just had on a T-shirt. The white lesions on her arms shone in the moonlight.

Slowly, gently, I touched her arm, right over the scars. The electricity was definitely back.

Max threw the hammer on the ground next to us. "I'm sorry for what I did to you," he said to me. "I still don't like you." He grinned at me. "But I'm glad we met."

"Likewise," I said, smiling back.

Max half-saluted us and walked away.

"Your grandma," Gramps said, standing next to us, "she cheated at Scrabble. Never would admit she was wrong. Not ever, even about the orange carpet. God, I miss her."

"I miss my brother," Jocelyn said. I had a feeling she had never actually said it out loud before.

"I miss who I used to be, when I wasn't scared all the time. When I wasn't trying so hard not to be angry," I found myself saying.

Jocelyn and I lay down on our backs again, staring up at the sky. She probably watched the stars. I looked up into blackness without blinking.

That's that. The next day, Dad finished the yard horse demolition. When he and Mom had come home from their date the night before and spotted us sprawled out around the broken yard horse, he hadn't even asked what happened. Just said, "I've always hated that freaking horse." He was grinning a little now as he whapped at the remains with a hammer in the morning light.

Across the street, Jocelyn waved as she and her mom got in their car. She was wearing a tank top. Later, I was going to ask her to go to the coffee shop with me. Like on a real date. Sort of, anyway, considering Mom or Dad would drive us there and pick us up.

I pulled my phone out of my pocket and banged out a quick text to Alice.

Knock, knock.

It took a few seconds—I knew she was at the animal hospital; Tooter couldn't seem to wake up that morning—but soon my phone dinged with a reply.

Who's there?

Me. In a couple days.

WHAT?!?

Mom's bringing me on Sunday. If you'd like some company.

After a few seconds, she replied.

Thank you.

I smiled, tucked the phone back in my pocket, and walked up toward the house.

"Gramps?" He had set up a lawn chair on the front porch to watch Dad take down the rest of the yard horse.

"Hmm?"

"Can we stay with you? I mean, if you don't mind, can we all live here with you? I haven't asked Mom and Dad yet, but I'd like to stay. Maybe finish high school here."

Gramps nodded. "I'd like that."

"But some things will have to change," I added.

"They always do." *Cah, cah, cah!*

So that's that, Dr. Thomas. I wrote it all down, just like you said, in the hopes that you can make me normal.

The thing is, Doc, even I can see (get it, see?) that there's no such thing. None of us are normal.

But I think we're going to be okay.

Acknowledgments

Thank you to my family and the baristas at my local Starbucks, both of whom politely ignored me randomly snorting laughter and ugly crying (sometimes both) while crafting Richie Ryder Raymond. Much love to super-agent Nicole Resciniti for falling in love with Richie's story and showing me how to make it even better. I'm so grateful! Just as much love to Julie Matysik, editor extraordinaire, for strengthening and polishing the Blind Guide series. Much gratitude to Kathryn Svendsen (Shelf Full of Books reviewer) for her insight on working with students who have limited vision.

Also, thanks to my parents' yard horse. Sorry we never dressed you up.